ECHO POINT

VIRGINIA HALE

BELLA
B O O K S

2017

Bella Books, Inc.
P.O. Box 10543
Tallahassee, FL 32302

Printed in the United States of America on acid-free paper.

First Bella Books Edition 2017

Editor: Ann Roberts
Cover Designer: Judith Fellows

ISBN: 978-1-59493-577-0

About the Author

Virginia Hale lives in Sydney, Australia, and is currently completing her M.A. in Children's Literature. When she isn't writing or studying, she is dreaming up trips to New York and Boston. *Echo Point*—set in the heartland of the Blue Mountains—is her debut novel.

Acknowledgments

Many thanks to my editor, Ann Roberts. Your support and advice has been tremendously helpful. To Jessica Hill and the staff at Bella Books, thank you for making this possible.

CHAPTER ONE

Bronwyn Lee was a woman on a mission. She pressed her cheek flush to the cool wooden floorboards and squinted into the dark void beneath her sister's dresser, praying to God she would spot a tiny glimmer. That iPhone torch app would have come in handy right about now, Bron thought, before reminding herself that her six-year-old niece Annie hadn't purposely dropped her phone the night before. The million shards of her phone screen across the kitchen floor weren't worth even one of Annie's guilty tears. Regardless, Annie had shed enough tears to buoy a naval ship.

Bron huffed and scooted closer. There was probably a torch in the shed outside, but asking her stepmother Jackie for the key to the shed would lead to nagging questions like, "Why do you need a torch?" or "What is it that you're looking for?" Bron didn't have the heart to tell her saintly stepmother she'd misplaced Libby's ring. Perhaps misplaced was a strong word. Bron couldn't be *completely* certain, but she was *almost* sure that she'd seen the ring in Libby's jewellery box three months prior when she first came home for Libby's funeral. She'd stumbled upon the ring and put it aside selfishly for safekeeping, knowing full well Libby would have liked to be buried with it on her finger.

Had she imagined finding the ring? Had she imagined the guilt? Had she dreamt it up on one of those jetlagged, grief-stricken nights after the accident?

The rim of her reading glasses tapped the ironbark floor. Frustrated, she slid the black frames to the crown of her head. It was like Ripley's *Believe it or Not!* Museum under the dresser. She couldn't see anything past the dusty fort of bobby pins, hair ties and cap-less, half-used lip balms she was sure Libby had unknowingly hoarded since their teenage years.

The grandfather clock chimed on the half hour. Bron stood up and threw her glasses onto Libby's freshly made bed. She ran a shaky hand across her face. They would all be back soon with Ally, and Bron would no longer have a chance to pull apart her sister's bedroom in search of the ring. As she blew back a few blond strands which had come loose from her ponytail, her gaze landed on one of the photographs on the dresser. The cheap frame held a picture of Libby, no older than fourteen, and Ally, her arm around Libby. Bron rubbed the pad of her thumb back and forth over the tarnished plate at the bottom of the frame, trying to buff up the first few engraved letters of "Two Peas in a Pod." She stared into her sister's adolescent grin and imagined what Libby would think of her quest to find the ring. How dare you not trust my best friend, Libby would chastise. But Bron had never trusted Ally—and Ally had never given her reason to. Bron couldn't bring herself to feel even a sliver of shame for judging the younger woman. The sad truth was Bron didn't doubt for a second that Ally wouldn't pawn Libby's ring the minute she laid eyes on it. Ally was reckless, wild and careless. *Uncontrollable.* Her recent track record said it all. Or rather, her parole agreement did.

Just the thought of that precious, albeit fairly inexpensive ring sitting in a glass case of a hockshop in Katoomba town centre made Bron dizzy with rage. She so clearly remembered the day she'd given Libby the ring for her twenty-first birthday. One day, way down the track, she could pass it on to Annie when she turned twenty-one, assuming she could actually find the cursed platinum band in the first place.

She'd already checked the dresser drawers, beneath the mattress, and the pockets of Libby's clothes, which Bron had shifted to her own closet that morning to give Ally her own space—even if it was in a room which smelled, looked and *felt* like Libby. Surely Ally would feel it too.

She'd casually asked Jackie about the ring the night before. "Mum, you know that ring I gave Libby? Did she wear it much?" Bron had paused. "She wasn't wearing it the day of the accident."

On her way to bed, Jackie had pressed her thin, tired frame against the doorjamb of Libby's bedroom, watching as Bron emptied the top drawer of Libby's bedside table. With a yawn, Jackie said she'd often seen the ring lying on the edge of the bathtub in the evening, or it would catch her eye in the morning as the sun streamed in through the kitchen window, the small, silver-encased diamond glittering next to the drying breakfast dishes Libby had washed before leaving for work. "When it wasn't on Libby's finger, it was lying around here somewhere, more often than not next to a drain," Jackie complained with a chuckle and nodded at the jewellery box across the room. "Did you see it in there?"

Bron had bitten the side of her cheek so hard she'd almost drawn blood. "Yep." It wasn't a lie. She had seen it. Possibly. Three months ago.

And that was that. Assuming the ring was safe in its jewellery box, Jackie had wished Bron a good night and retired to her bedroom down the hall. Bron had stood there, cursing herself for not placing it somewhere safe the first time she'd seen it. Well, the first time she *may* have seen it. Without Jackie's help, she was out of options. She didn't expect Daniel, her twenty-three-year-old half-brother, to remember a detail as small as the ring on their sister's finger. She wanted to ask Annie about it. Of course, she wouldn't be in trouble if she'd taken it, but

Bron knew it was unlikely. She hadn't seen the little girl go near Libby's bedroom in months.

Bron looked around the room hopelessly. If she couldn't find it turning Libby's room upside down, there was little chance Ally would. Better to leave it be, she decided, than to worry her mother or brother over something so materialistic. It was the concern that weighed on her mind each time she thought of the ring—she would seem petty to her family. She'd just lost her beautiful baby sister to a freak car accident, and she was worried about an old ring with a diamond hardly bigger than a grain of sand? Maybe this was the universe's way of forcing her to readjust her priorities. Perhaps it was perspective, not diamonds, that was a girl's best friend.

She saw them before she heard them. Through the thin curtains of Libby's bedroom window, she watched the red Toyota—so old it had served as her very first car—stall at the gate. At the very end of the driveway, past the blue gum trees, she could make out the tall figure of her brother opening the front gate, shooing a barking Tammy away from the gravel path. The familiar, heavy slam of the driver's door as he got back in reached Bron's ears through the open window.

They drove toward the house, the golden retriever chasing after them. Bron watched Jackie turn around in the front seat and throw her head back in laughter, probably at something Annie had asked in that painfully earnest manner that only little kids can get away with. Or, quite possibly, Jackie was laughing at Ally.

Sweet, forgiving Jackie had always loved Ally as much as her own children—step-daughters too. Jackie had never made Bron or Libby feel any less her children than Daniel. Daniel, a product of Bron's father's second marriage to Jackie, was barely crawling when Libby started fifth grade. At that point, Bron, two years from graduating high school, had initially thought it a blessing when Libby began bringing Ally Shepherd around for dinner, sleepovers, or a swim in the snake-ridden swamp out back—much to Jackie's terror and their father's indifference. Bron already had so much on her plate—a part-time job at the bakery, helping Jackie with Daniel, and trying to finish school with grades good enough to take her to all of the places she wanted to go. Finding time to entertain her ten-year-old sister was no longer a priority. But Jackie fawned over Libby's new friend, and it had sparked Bron's jealousy, despite her being seventeen. After only a few months into Libby and Ally's friendship, Ally would show up uninvited on their doorstep after dinner, as though Jackie hadn't had enough on her plate with a toddler, two teenage girls, and their impatient, stubborn father. Their father had called Ally one of the Lost Girls, always believing Ally's penchant for endlessly running away from home was juvenile. They all had—at first.

In hindsight, Bron could see she'd been jealous of Ally. After losing her own mother to a heart attack when Bron was fourteen and Libby just seven—*god, just a year older than Annie*—Bron's desire for Jackie's maternal attention had grown. And by simply asking Jackie for another glass of cordial or to stay the night, ten-year-old Ally had struck a nerve in seventeen-year-old Bron.

The Toyota drew to a stop in its usual place just off the circular driveway in front of their two-story Colonial Queenslander. Annie was the first one out of the car, bouncing up the front steps of the wraparound veranda and out of Bron's line of sight. Not a second later, Annie's high-pitched voice rang out from downstairs, "Aunty Bron, we're home!"

Bron jumped as the front door banged dramatically against the bulky iron doorstop. "Ah, shit," she heard the six-year-old curse quietly. Still focused on the car, Bron rolled her eyes. She'd berated Annie for swearing more times than Jackie had chided her for swinging open the front door too harshly. It was like a never-ending cycle: door crashed, Nanna screamed, Annie swore, and Aunt Bron went bananas. Each time it occurred, Bron grew increasingly concerned about her new role as Annie's guardian.

She shifted back from the open window and watched her brother, mother and Ally deep in conversation. Ally's head was turned and it was hard to get a good look at her from Bron's vantage point, especially with the way the shadow from the veranda roof leaked over the windscreen. Bron moved to the next window, where she could clearly make out Jackie, leaning forward from the backseat. She said something, which prompted Ally to nod slowly, and then Jackie gripped the juncture of Ally's neck and shoulder reassuringly. So often Jackie had squeezed Bron's shoulder comfortingly in the last few months that, standing there at Libby's bedroom window, Bron felt it like a phantom caress.

Annie's rubber thongs hesitantly flipped and flopped their way up the stairs. "Did you hear that?" Annie asked meekly from the doorway.

"Did I hear what?" Focused on the car, Bron raised a knowing eyebrow.

In the reflection of Libby's dressing table mirror, she watched Annie bite her lip in an attempt to stifle a laugh. With one last glance down at the car, she crossed the room and playfully snaked her fingers beneath Annie's armpits. She hoisted her petite frame onto her hip. Annie struggled against her, laughing.

"If I hear you swear one more time today, I'll empty the water that's left in the baby pool onto Nanna's lettuce bed and you won't swim for a week."

"Okay, okay! Please put me down!" Annie groaned as Bron padded down the stairs, ignoring the request. "Aunty Bron, please!" she begged, pressing the palms of her hands into the hollow of Bron's cheeks, the ridges of her cheekbones more prominent than they'd been months ago. "Youse is so bony and it's real hot!"

"You're, not 'youse'," Bron corrected. "Ewes are female sheep." She sighed deeply, knowing her efforts were possibly in vain. When she returned to Boston—even if it was just to finalize her affairs—and Annie was left under Daniel and Jackie's influence, Annie would slip deeper into that cringe-worthy rural Australian dialect.

A familiar, raspy voice floated in on the stifling breeze coming through the open front door. A car door shut and then another. Bron could faintly make out Daniel's insistence to bring Ally's bags inside and then the squeak of the car boot opening.

With the hand that wasn't supporting Annie, Bron picked at the thin, dampened cotton between her breasts and ignored the anticipatory flush that broke over her skin.

Ally stepped through the front door first and stopped abruptly when she saw Bron at the base of the staircase. She seemed to struggle for a second, as though she wanted to start with something simple, like hello or how are you? For a second—a split second, really—Bron almost felt sorry for Ally, until her pained expression brightened into that familiar Ally smirk, complete with a raised eyebrow and a single, gorgeously smug dimple.

Annie squirmed against Bron's side. "Ew, you got sweat on your lip," she whined.

The smirk split across Ally's face into a full-fledged grin. Features Bron remembered as somewhat angular were now sharp. Ally's cheekbones were more defined than Bron's, her jawline pronounced. Bron had expected her to be…more solid. Ally was almost stick thin, as though she hadn't eaten properly in weeks. But there was something about the darkness in her eyes—so strangely alike to Libby's glossy chestnut stare—which eliminated any thought of Ally as frail. If Bron once thought the mere presence of this girl intense, the woman standing before her now was…something else, something entirely new to contend with. At thirty-three, Ally Shepherd was all grown up.

Bron set Annie down, and took in the faded green tattoo sleeve that decorated Ally's right arm from shoulder to elbow. Typical, Bron thought to herself.

She hadn't seen Ally since before she left for America. Then, Ally had been barely…twenty-two, perhaps? It had only been three months later when Libby had phoned in tears, telling Bron about the video store robbery, and that, of course, like the time before that, Ally was innocent. Libby had rattled off a number of defences then: Ally was just in the wrong place at the wrong time, Ally had just lost her dad, Ally's family's motel business was going under, and Ally's mother was still refusing to even entertain the idea that Ally was a lesbian. But this time Libby must have known the truth. In her tiny Back Bay apartment, waiting for Libby's inevitable request to wire bail money for Ally, Bron had angrily held the landline so tightly to her ear that her hand had cramped. But the request hadn't come. Apparently, Bron wasn't the only Lee sister who'd had the last straw with Ally Shepherd.

Now, standing in the hallway, four inches taller than Bron, Ally was older and very much a grown woman. Bron wondered if she was grateful for another chance—or if it was simply just expected.

They were quiet, listening as Jackie's and Dan's voices moved around the back of the house, pandering in baby voices to Tammy's howls of disappointment at Ally's sudden disappearance inside. "Where's she gone, Tam?" Daniel asked the dog. "Where's Al gone?"

Bron looked down at her niece. "Go open the back door for Nanna, please."

As Annie ran off, Ally's gaze unabashedly dropped to Bron's legs, bare in her short denim cut-offs.

"I'm jealous," Ally smirked playfully.

Bron quickly licked her lips and shoved her left hand into a pocket of her shorts. "Pardon?" she prompted curtly, hoping the way she leaned against the banister looked as casual as intended.

Ally gestured to her own tight, dark denim jeans. "Next time I decide to spend a five-year holiday behind bars, I'll be sure to commit a crime that'll land me there long enough to leave the same season I go in. It's a fuckin' sweat bath down here." Bron tried not to flinch at the profanity, watching intently as Ally ran a hand through her short-cropped, ebony black hair. Ally pinched the material at her thigh. "Thought about chopping these off at the knee."

Bron pursed her lips. "It's quite hot. We're expecting bushfires relatively soon."

Ally gasped dramatically and her eyes widened playfully in that sarcastic way that had always been so, so Ally. "Well, good thing I'm here now. I was a firey," she pointed out cockily. "Pretty sure you remember, Bron."

She did. Ally's past as a volunteer firefighter had been perhaps her single redeeming quality. "Yes, well…bushfires aren't anything to joke about," Bron admonished.

Ally's expression hazed over. "You think you need to lecture *me* about bushfires?"

She swallowed in sudden recollection. Her face grew hot at the faux pas and the back of her neck burned uncomfortably. Yes, Ally knew all about fire.

There was that cocky grin again, glazing its way across Ally's face. "Maybe one day, if you're lucky," Ally rasped, "I'll show you the scars."

"I see you haven't lost that sense of humour Libby was so fond of."

"I see you haven't lost your Aussie accent. I was worried you were going to sound like a Yank."

The screen door at the back of the house squeaked open. "Bron! Al's here!" Jackie's voice rang out before she stepped into the hall. "Oh! You found her." She gestured toward the kitchen. "Come in here and have a cold drink."

Ally held Bron's stare for a moment before following Jackie.

Daniel held up a small bag. "You want this upstairs, Al?"

Ally hesitated and she looked to Jackie.

"We've put you in Lib's old room," Jackie said into the fridge. "You don't mind?"

Reaching into the cupboard for five glasses, Bron watched Ally's expression in the reflection of the oven glass across the room.

"No," Ally replied lowly. "Lib's room is fine." She cleared her throat as she took a seat at the kitchen table.

Daniel swung the small gym bag full of Ally's belongings over his shoulder. It was evidently half-empty, the cracking vinyl sunken at its sides. Roughing her hair up, he bent down to kiss the top of her head.

"Get off," Ally laughed, pushing him away as he took off down the hall.

Bron set the glasses down for Jackie, contemplating the exchange with guarded amusement, trying to remember the last time her brother had been comfortable enough to be so playful with her. She pulled out a chair at the end of the table and sat back.

Ally smiled at her and Bron crossed her legs.

"Lemonade good?" Jackie asked Ally, already pouring her a glass from the plastic Schweppes bottle. She slid the fizzing drink in front of Ally.

"Thanks, Jacs."

Bron took her in. The way Ally held herself was…captivating. The way she splayed herself out in the kitchen chair, relaxed and comfortable, commanded the attention of everybody in the room. At least, it commanded Bron's attention. Jackie was preoccupied, shouting instructions out the backdoor for Annie to wash up for dinner.

She watched, irritably, as Ally twisted her glass of lemonade, swirling the ring of condensation across the wooden tabletop. She was completely unapologetic for the grief she had caused this family—a family that wasn't even hers. Bron imagined Ally's legs, spread apart with the impropriety of a teenage boy. She could almost remember the way Ally's knees used to tap against hers at dinner when they were kids…

"God," the rough timber of Ally's voice started. "Haven't seen you since before Annie was born. It must have been Christmas of…what…'06?"

Bron looked up, the realisation suddenly dawning upon her that Ally's question was directed at her.

"Before that I think."

"Bet Boston's missing you."

Bron forced a smile, surprised that Ally seemed to care enough to remember where she now called home. "It is."

She wasn't going to give Ally any more than that, not when her parole was the main reason Bron still found herself in the mountains, three months after Libby's funeral and well into the hot Australian summer.

Bron loathed the Australian summer. The week before, temperatures had spiked to forty degrees Celsius, and she'd dreamed about a snow-clad Boston Common. She'd woken in a sweat, the old rainbow ribbons her newly out-and-proud twenty-year-old self had tied to the bars of her fan fluttering weakly on the pathetic, oscillating breeze. But the night after that had been unbearable. Annie had climbed into her bed midmorning, and Bron, alien to the uninhibited nature of a sleeping child, had laid awake, sweltering as her unconscious niece threw her limbs across the mattress and her aunt like a possessed ragdoll. When Bron finally dozed off around four a.m., she'd had another nightmare: herself, floating naked in Boston's very shallow and very public Copley Square fountain in broad daylight.

Clearly uncomfortable under Bron's scrutiny, Ally watched Jackie chase Annie into the laundry to wash her hands for lunch. When Jackie disappeared, Ally craned her neck backward, looking to the stairs for Dan.

Even with a wall between them, Bron knew the second Jackie turned on the high wash tub tap for Annie. The old pipes shuddered violently in the wall between the kitchen and laundry, so much so that Ally flinched, until she put two and two together. Bron would call a plumber to look at the problem before she left for Boston. On just a pension, Jackie had been struggling to make ends meet since her retirement. When Bron had first arrived home, she'd caught Jackie adding water to her jar of anti-ageing face cream to make it go further. That week, as she shopped for groceries in a grief-induced haze, Bron had bought the store out of the face cream in Jackie's favourite brand.

Ally caught Bron's gaze again. "How long are you here for?"

"Depends." *On how long it takes me to trust that you won't do anything stupid when I leave you here with my family.*

Ally motioned to the wheezing fan on top of the fridge. "That fan's not doing a whole lot for us."

"My apologies if the air-conditioning system in Oberon Women's Correctional Centre is more to your liking than our ancient appliances." It hadn't meant to come out so biting. Bron added a chuckle to soften the blow.

Ally placed her hands behind her head, sat back even further in the chair, and clicked her tongue playfully. Bron tried to shift in her seat, too, but in the heat, the backs of her thighs had already glued themselves to the vinyl base.

"Hey, Ally!" Annie called, steered into the kitchen by Nanna Jackie rubbing vigorously at Annie's drenched forearms with a hand towel. "You know what I found out while I was washing my hands? Your name is just like mine but you got two Ls and I got two Ns. And I got an *ie* and you got a *y*. But it don't matter 'cause they mostly sound the same, yeah? We're like twins!"

"We are," Ally agreed. "Want to see something cool?"

Annie nodded.

Ally pulled down the right band of her tank top, baring her black bra strap.

Bron raised an eyebrow at Ally's blatant immodesty, averting her gaze, not giving Ally the satisfaction of appearing startled. Until she saw it. An angry red welt of fresh prison ink.

"That's my name," Annie said in wonder, her little fingertips scanning the letters that travelled at least four inches across the right side of Ally's chest.

Bron fought the urge to roll her eyes. She'd never seen anything so ridiculous in her life. She'd thought parents who got the names of their kids tattooed on their bodies was stupid, but this was something else.

And then it dawned on her. What better way for Ally to weave her way into this family? If she screwed up, made one wrong turn, Bron knew Ally would play the Annie card to get back into Jackie's good graces. The contract was inked into her skin. The tattoo may have appeared to be healing—a week old at most—but the whole thing just screamed infection.

Annie was off on a roll of interview questions: Had it hurt? Had she cried? Did it still hurt? No? Who did it? Ally did it *herself*? She was so brave. It seemed Annie had found a new toy to play with. Boring Aunt Bron the children's book illustrator paled in comparison to decorated deviant Ally.

"Uncle Dan, look," Annie instructed as Daniel reached into the fridge and pulled out a beer.

"Wow," Daniel remarked, surprised. "That's super nice."

"She did it herself," Annie informed him.

Pulling out one of the kitchen chairs, Daniel visibly cringed at the redness of Ally's skin. "I wouldn't do that, not even for you, Ann."

Bron sipped her lemonade between clenched teeth as she listened to Ally and her brother talk about their plans for the upcoming work week—how many homeowners had booked Daniel for painting jobs and how many quotes they'd give before the end of the week. Weeks before, Ally had taken up Daniel's offer to work in his business to satisfy the requirements of her parole agreement. Bron hoped to God that Ally wouldn't do anything to jeopardise Daniel's reputation as one of the finest house painters in Katoomba.

With a quick glance around the room to see if anyone was watching her, Annie stood up on her chair, turned to the fan, and drew her singlet up over her head, clearly as bored with the conversation as Bron was. The vinyl squeaked as her tiny feet twisted on the clammy surface. "It's so hot, Ally!" Annie sighed deeply, throwing her singlet to the floor.

"Be careful," Bron instructed.

"Remind you of someone?" Jackie wiggled her eyebrows at Ally.

Ally grinned. "Yep."

"Did you have a swimming pool in prison?" Annie wondered, the golden blond strands of her long hair flying about her doll-like face.

Bron let out a chuckle.

Ally shot Bron a pointed stare. "No, babe," she answered, her gaze locked on Bron, "but I took a lot of nice long cold showers."

"Well, bad luck for you then," Annie sighed. "Uncle Dan only lets us have two-minute showers 'cause there's pretty much no water 'cause of the drought! Better go back to prison!"

"Annie!" Jackie reprimanded.

"What?"

"That was rude!"

"I was only joking!"

Bron cleared her throat. "Annie, can you do me a favour and go pop some ice from the back fridge into Tammy's bucket?"

Annie sighed. "'Kay, but I'm not putting my shirt back on. Too hot."

Bron smiled softly. "Deal."

"She's been a bit mouthy since the accident," Jackie whispered when they heard the suction of the back fridge pop. "Just tell her off if she gets smart with you."

"She's all right," Ally said, brushing Annie's rudeness aside.

Jackie shook her head. "She needs to be put back in her place."

Bron couldn't help but pipe up. "Her psychologist says it's completely normal. Expected, even. She was in a car accident and she lost her mother. Give her a break, Mum."

Jackie took a seat at the table. "And what do you think Lib would have to say about the cheek she's been giving?"

"Libby had a mouth on her," Ally cut in. "And she turned out just fine."

"Annie *doesn't* have a mouth on her," Bron insisted.

"I remember when Libby came to bail me out...the first time," Ally chuckled.

Dan must have kicked Ally under the table, because suddenly they were both laughing and Jackie was telling them to stop mucking around. Suddenly Bron felt like she had no place in this comfortable, relaxed family dynamic.

"Anyway," Ally continued, "as I was saying before I was rudely interrupted," she said with a wink at Dan, "Lib gave the screw so much shit that the fucker decided to leave me in there three hours after she handed over the cash. I could hear her from out back. Can still hear her. 'I went all the way into town to take out two bloody grand and you're still givin' me shit.'"

Jackie and Dan laughed politely, but the room slowly fell silent. They all listened to Annie's distant voice instructing Tammy. "Drink ya water, matey."

"I never did pay Lib back that bail money," Ally whispered, her eyes fixed on the bottom of her glass.

Jackie reached for Ally's hand and squeezed her fingers. "Love, what's done is done. She wouldn't have minded… wouldn't have given it a second thought."

"I wouldn't worry," Bron interrupted. "It wasn't Libby's money."

Ally looked up. "Huh?"

Bron had waited twenty-three years for this moment. "It was my money she used to bail you out." She let her words sink in for a moment before she added, "The first time."

Ally squirmed and sat up a little straighter. "It was yours?"

"Uh-huh. And it wasn't two grand. It was three grand she borrowed from me. *I* drove her into town, and I took the money out on *my* credit card."

For a long moment, nobody said anything.

"You were paying off uni as you went. Where the hell did you get three grand?" Jackie wondered, her greying eyebrows fussing together with worry.

"The money I'd been saving for New York. Plus some more I took out on credit."

At the other end of the table, the tendons in Ally's neck tensed.

"Never mind," Bron muttered. "A year later, I had it back."

Ally's gaze shot up again. "So she paid you back?" she asked, relieved.

How convenient, Bron considered, for Ally to think her debt died with loyal, hard-working Libby. Bron leaned forward in her chair and ran her finger along the rim of her glass. "No. After approximately two hundred four a.m. bakery shifts I had it back."

She met Ally's stare. The wooden legs of Ally's chair screeched as she stood up. She pushed it back under the table roughly. In a second, she was gone from the room.

"Why can't you just let it go?" Dan huffed.

She shrugged and glanced at Jackie. The pain and disappointment swimming in greyish-blue eyes made her look away quickly.

Heavy boots pounded back down the stairs.

Bron jumped when Ally slammed her hand—and a small wad of fresh, crisp fifty-dollar notes—down on the kitchen table in front of her. "There's three hundred to start and I'll get you the rest next week," Ally rasped.

Bron swallowed nervously, thrown off her game.

Ally kicked her chair back out and slid down into it, her arms crossed tightly across her full breasts, across the tattoo. "Just let me know how much interest you've calculated over the years, Bron," Ally spat. "Because clearly, you've given it a lot of thought."

CHAPTER TWO

The headlights of a neighbour's car returning home threw a weak glow along the path of the pitch-black driveway. With Tammy under her feet, Bron's toes gripped her thongs tighter as she watched her step down the steepest part of the driveway. How on earth had they sped down it on their bikes every day as kids and not *once* toppled over the handlebars?

She held Daniel's phone up, knowing she most likely wouldn't be able to get a decent signal until she reached the gate. Two bars of reception—enough to call an ambulance, but not enough to check the messages left on her home phone in Boston. She groaned, picturing her shattered phone again.

She smiled at the home screen of Daniel's phone, his girlfriend Carly, beaming, at her university graduation last month. Daniel's arm wrapped around her robed shoulders, pretending to bite at the gold tassel of her graduation cap. Despite his childishness in the picture, the suited man in the picture was anything but immature.

The last time Bron had been home, Daniel had been studying for his Higher School Certificate. Now twenty-three, he had his own painting business and was off every night with Carly. They seemed serious but Jackie had a different impression, which she'd expressed to Bron in confidence. Carly was already furthering her studies in graduate school in the city, while Daniel was a painter with a backup plan to head out further west rather than coastal east if there was ever a shortage of work in the mountains. They wouldn't last, Jackie believed. But to Bron they seemed happy, in love, and as depressing as it seemed, mature enough to make sacrifices for each other. She wouldn't be surprised if they were engaged by Christmas. There's an eighteen-year age difference between us, Bron thought, and yet I've never had a relationship based on mutual compromise.

Bron doubted forty was going to be her lucky year in the romance department, because it had been miserable in every other respect. Since losing Libby, things had been on a downward spiral. The first challenge had been getting Annie's grief and anxiety under control—doctor's appointments, counselling appointments, spending the first few hours of each Monday morning in Annie's kindergarten classroom until she'd adjusted enough to let Bron leave without having a meltdown. Bron's commitment to her family meant not only had she been forced to postpone the start of her new project with Yellowstone Books, she'd also had to ask MIT for additional time to think over their teaching job offer. And just when things had finally been getting back on track, Rae had decided to call things off with her, a month from their one-year anniversary.

And now there was Ally.

As she locked the home screen, she took note of the time. Three minutes from eleven and Ally still wasn't home. Bron had been stupid to think there was even a remote possibility that Ally would respect her curfew—and Bron.

Ally had washed and wiped up after dinner, bragging all the while about the autonomy the officers had granted her in the prison kitchen. After being thanked profusely by Jackie for refusing to allow anybody else to clean up, Ally pulled the first payback card.

"I'm going to take a walk."

All three adults in the room spun around to look at the clock. 9:36. Exactly twenty-four minutes until curfew. The rule was outlined on the second page of her parole agreement.

"Can I come?" Annie begged, heartbroken when Bron told her it was *way* past her bedtime, and then instructed her to go and change into her pyjamas and brush her teeth.

"Well don't be long," Jackie urged Ally.

As Bron tucked Annie into bed and kissed her goodnight, she watched from Annie's bedroom window as Ally closed the front gate at the end of the driveway, leaving a whimpering Tammy inside, and headed in the direction of Katoomba town centre.

An hour and a half later, she still wasn't home. Bron was anxious. Jackie had been the one to write the letter of commitment to help Ally in her reintroduction to society. Along with their address, Jackie's name and the signed letter were in the parole plan. Since Jackie wasn't able to drive the streets in the dark in search of Ally, was it Bron's responsibility? Could she get into trouble if Ally's parole officer somehow found out that Ally had breached parole?

She kicked at a rock on the path and Tammy chased it. She tried to imagine where Ally might have taken herself on foot. Echo Point, the popular tourist lookout, was a far distance from the end of the main street of Katoomba. Although the time of night would blanket the green valley in complete darkness, the view from the cliff-top platform was nothing short of magical— The Three Sisters, set against the blackness of the night sky, illuminated from below by hugely powered lights, their brown rock faces almost golden.

It was stunning at night, but Bron preferred the rock formation in daylight. If she ventured down there tomorrow, right at the crack of dawn before the heat set in and the busloads of tourists arrived, she would be able to see the silver mist the eucalyptus trees breathed across the canyon, giving the Blue Mountains its colourful namesake. There was something calm about the view from the top. The day after Libby's funeral, Bron had taken Annie down to the lookout, the two of them bundled up in beanies and scarves. She had given her orphaned niece two dollars to keep her occupied with one of the telescopes, and then leaned against the railing, looking out at The Three Sisters and thinking about how there had once been seven, and how they'd eroded away long ago.

Reaching the gate, Bron watched another reception bar light up. Three bars. It wasn't going to get much better than that. She wasn't surprised to hear the monotonous recording inform her that she had three new messages since she hadn't bothered to dial through for at least a week. She deleted the first two, old work messages she'd already received via email. The third was a charity she'd donated to months ago and would undoubtedly hear from for the rest of her life. Like last week, there was nothing from Rae. Bron didn't know how she felt about that.

"Calling the cops on me?"

She pivoted on the spot. Ally shut the gate behind her and crouched down to roughhouse with Tammy. Bron's gaze dropped to Ally's thighs. Lean muscle strained against the unhemmed, fraying line of her shorts, which two hours before had been jeans. Bron rolled her eyes and hung up on the message service.

"Enjoy your walk?" she asked sarcastically.

"Yep," Ally played. "I expected you to wait up for me, but you didn't have to come all the way out here—"

"Look, mind your curfew next time. Aren't you grateful you can serve the last two years of your sentence in relative freedom? Pulling crap like what you've done tonight… It's not fair to us when we've just gone and stuck our necks out for you, okay? I don't appreciate being played."

Ally straightened. "Okay. Sorry," she added reluctantly. "I'm not playing games."

Bron couldn't be bothered starting another argument, so she started the uphill walk back to the house, Ally falling in step beside her. Considering Ally thought she'd been down by the gate waiting for her, Bron said, "There's no reception up at the house. I had to check my messages on Daniel's phone since mine is broken."

"Yeah, Daniel told me. Did you need to call the boyfriend?"

She slowed. "Excuse me?" she asked in utter confusion, her gaze searching Ally's face for any hint of jest.

Ally looked down at her, her face blank. "What?"

Bron shook her head. How on earth had their signals crossed so spectacularly? Sudden, deep upset erupted within her. Had the entire family managed to conveniently omit the minor detail that she'd been dating women since...forever? "I...I don't have a boyfriend."

A slow smirk broke out on Ally's face. "I'm fucking with you, Bron. Libby told me you're a dyke ages ago, like back in the Stone Age."

Bron didn't know which maddened her more—Ally's knack for catching her off guard, or Ally rekindling the horrible sadness invoked by Bron's family's resistance to her sexual identity. She pursed her lips and picked up the pace.

"I've known a lot longer than Lib, though," Ally continued. "I watched you check out *Desert Hearts* from the video store every second weekend."

"Twice. I only rented it twice."

Ally chuckled. "Well, I think the Michelle Pfeiffer Catwoman poster on your bedroom wall gave you away too. I figured it was either narcissism or lesbianism that made you pin it up."

"Narcissism?"

"I've always thought you look just like her. Blue eyes, blond hair. Pint-sized, but just like her."

"Oh. Well...thank you."

When the silence that had settled upon them obviously began to make her uncomfortable, Ally spoke up. "So the main street is still pretty much the same."

She hummed her disagreement. "Something's always different each time I come home."

"How often is that?"

"Up until now? Every three years or so."

"I've been away four. Still looks the same to me."

Don't bite, don't bite...

"I *am* surprised to see there are still three sisters. Felt like I'd been in for so long, that there'd only be one left by the time I got out."

So she *had* been down to the lookout, not town, not her mother's house.

"Look," Ally started, pinching at the bottom of her singlet in an invitation to the cooling breeze. "About the money—"

Bron sighed. "We can figure it out later, Ally."

She raised an eyebrow. "Sure?"

Running a hand through her hair, Bron nodded.

"Your hair is longer," Ally commented. "Haven't seen it so long in a while."

At the certainty that Ally's gaze was on her, apprehension broke across Bron's skin, hot and unwarranted. When they reached the front steps, Ally reached out and grabbed the back of Bron's elbow. Her grip was firm, her eyes glassy. She licked her lips. "Can I ask you something?"

"Yes?"

Ally paused at the granted permission. Bron's gaze fell lower to where the tendons in her throat tensed. "Where is Libby?"

"The Anglican Cemetery in Leura," Bron said, softly.

"The one on the back road?"

"Yes. She's next to Mum and Dad."

"Can you…Do you think you could take me there sometime this week?"

Her anxiety prickled at the request. Although Jackie had taken Annie each weekend since the funeral, Bron hadn't been to Libby's grave since she watched her brother and uncles lower Libby into the ground.

"The grave…It's a bit of a mess. We had a few weeks of rain. It's sinking. We've been adding bags of potting mix every week or so, but it's a matter of just…waiting for the grass to grow. Mum asked the groundskeepers to have a look and see what they could do, but the morons just went and dumped huge clumps of clay on top. That only made it worse. The headstone isn't in yet either." She paused. "Maybe you should wait a bit."

"I don't mind," Ally assured her. "I'd like to go sooner than later."

Bron nodded. "I'll take you on Sunday."

"I'd really appreciate that." Ally's unfocused gaze dropped to where her fingers had lightly wrapped themselves around Bron's wrist. "Sorry," she said, jerking her hand away.

Quietly, they made their way inside. In the semidarkness of the end of the hall, Bron locked the front door behind them. As Ally stood beside her, bent over at the waist and peeling off her boots, Bron inhaled her scent. It wasn't perfume, of course. It was maybe cocoa butter or vanilla. Something else too. She couldn't place it, and she couldn't remember it.

Bron guessed Ally had recently had a haircut, judging by the short, clean hairline at the back of her neck. Her gaze ran over Ally's muscular back, admiring the prominent vertebrae—one, two, three—until they disappeared beneath the singlet. Her skin was firm. Lovely. The sudden impulse to reach out and touch it made the hairs stand up at the back of her own neck, and she quickly looked away.

"I might have a shower if that's okay," Ally whispered as she dropped her boots at the mat next to the infamous iron doorstop.

"Yep," Bron said shortly, kicking off her thongs. "Night."

The kitchen light trickled through the house. Barefoot, Bron padded down the hall, the floorboards cool beneath her feet. Jackie sat at the kitchen table in her nightgown, studying a barely inked crossword. She had moved the fan down from the fridge, and it wheezed on the table in front of her, the corners of the magazine flapping as the fan oscillated. Bron leaned against the cool doorframe and crossed her arms.

"Get reception?" Jackie asked.

Her pen met the paper forcefully as she scribbled each letter into the boxes of a vertical column. A wave of guilt flushed over Bron. Upsetting her mother brought her no pleasure. "Better than last night."

"Want a cuppa?" Jackie asked, still refusing to look up from the magazine.

"Nah, I'm off to bed. Just wanted to say goodnight."

"Night, then."

She waited for a moment, and when it was obvious Jackie wasn't about to start on her about the money fiasco earlier, she turned to leave.

"What's a twelve letter word for judgmental?" Jackie murmured. "Starts with *s*."

She tapped her slim fingers against the doorframe, thinking. "Supercilious?"

Jackie glanced up over the rim over her glasses.

She rolled her eyes, feeling ridiculous. "Okay. Good one. I hear you. I'm exhausted."

"Bron…"

"What?"

"Are you going to apologise to Ally?"

She ran her tongue along the front of her teeth and appraised her stepmother. "Maybe."

Jackie looked back down at the page, obviously unamused.

"Mum?"

"Yeah, darl?"

She swallowed over the lump in her throat. "I can't find Libby's ring. I'm almost certain it was in her jewellery box, but it's not there anymore."

Jackie set her pen down and pushed her reading glasses up onto her head. "The one you gave her?"

Bron nodded.

"Do you think Annie has it?"

"I have no idea. I don't think so."

"It'll turn up, Bron."

"Yeah. Night, Mum."

"Night, love."

She laid awake long enough to see the red digits of her bedside clock flick over to three thirty-two a.m. She rolled over for what felt like the hundredth time and realized she could hear footsteps—tiny footsteps—making their way down the hall. She smoothed her hand over the cold top sheet and waited for her door to creak open.

It was funny the way her heart had learned to swell at the anticipation of *Annie*. Energetic Annie after school in the playground, sleepy Annie at the breakfast table, or frustrated, exhausted Annie in the early hours of the morning.

But her door didn't open. Footsteps continued down the end of the hall, to Libby's old room.

"Annie?" Ally whispered through the wall, her voice hoarse with sleep.

"My room's real hot," Annie groaned loudly and Ally shushed her.

"Can I sleep in Mummy's room with you?"

Bron raised an eyebrow at her niece's carefully executed, guilt-trip of a question before the muffled voices went quiet.

Bron sat up, breathing a sigh of relief as a cool, early morning southerly washed over her clammy skin. A flutter on her work desk caught her eye. With the window open, her draft pages were catching flight.

She threw back the covers and picked up Page Two from the rug. She looked down at the draft. She wasn't happy with it—at all. What on earth had the art history department at MIT been thinking when they'd selected her teaching application? She'd drawn with more imagination and precision in her first year of university. There was still so much work to do before she could post first draft photocopies to the city on Friday afternoon.

She pinned the pages down with one of the snow globes she'd taken from Libby's room when she'd cleaned it out for Ally. The ornament was so old that the water had marked a putrid brown circular stain at the top of the globe. She remembered buying it on her first trip to New York. She remembered wrapping it in three pairs of socks, shoving those socks into the epicentre of her enormous suitcase, hoping that the souvenir wouldn't break before she got it home to her little sister. She shook it. The discoloured, once-white flakes were stuck, clumped where miniature Radio City Music Hall met inch-long Central Park.

Just as the breeze picked up, she heard giggling from Libby's bedroom. She sighed, irritated by the way her body betrayed her and allowed the sting of rejection to cramp in her chest. Pressing a hand against the fly screen to ensure it had no intention of dislodging and sailing down to the veranda like it had the week before, she gathered her hair to one side and sank back into her age-old mattress.

Everything was still the same as it had been yesterday, and at the same time, it was all so different. The ageing house still creaked with the swelling heat, and those god-awful rainbow ribbons still floated on humid air. But with Ally's arrival everything had been thrown off balance, and Bron wasn't sure she could find her way back to the careful routine she'd spent every ounce of her energy creating the last few months. Intuition and its ugly twin, experience, pestered her mind, slurring that history was going to repeat itself. Bedtimes and curfews were going to be the very least of her worries.

CHAPTER THREE

When Bron finally rolled out of bed just after seven, the house was rowdier than usual. She could hear Daniel loading up for work, paint cans clunking around each time he added something into the aluminium tray of the utility truck. In the kitchen directly below her bedroom, someone was chatting with Annie, but the voice was too muffled for her to be certain if it belonged to Ally or Jackie. She allowed herself a moment longer in bed, hoping that sixty seconds of indulgence would fuel her for the next sixteen hours.

Her gaze caught on the clothes rack in the corner of her bedroom. A multitude of Libby's skirts and dresses hung there, crammed together so they would all fit on the rail. Bron remembered a few. There was the silver velour dress Libby had worn to her high school formal, preserved in its plastic cover. At the other end of the rack was the tacky, white leather skirt Libby had paid a fortune for down in Sydney when she was fifteen, only to get it home and be told by their father that it was far too indecent to be worn in public. The skirt probably still had its original tag. Bron smiled to herself and stretched across the mattress in an attempt to wake up.

Pulling her hair into a bun, she moved to the rack. Just as she assumed, the skirt still had its tag attached. $167. She rolled her eyes and pulled at the skirt of one of the sundresses, gathering the thin cotton to her face. Arrested by the scent of Libby's perfume, of just *Libby*, her eyes watered.

Downstairs, there was laughter, loud, brash laughter—Ally, undoubtedly. Tammy barked from outside, thrilled by so much commotion at such an early hour.

The thin, cardboard tag of another dress nicked the knuckle of her little finger. She brought the paper cut to her lips and grimaced at the metallic taste. She searched through the rack for the culprit that the tag belonged to—a dark green sundress. Brand new.

She pulled it out and appraised it. She *occasionally* wore a dress. This one was fairly plain and yet nicer than anything else she'd thrown into her suitcase. She couldn't exactly wear denim shorts to her meeting that afternoon, and shopping for anything but groceries was the last thing she wanted to do. She sighed, pulling the dress from its padded hanger.

Beneath the spray of the shower, she wondered how she would ever sort through all of Libby's clothes to give to charity. Beside the clothes rack at the end of her bed, there was still the cupboard in Libby's room she hadn't bothered cleaning out, and there was a lowboy full of winter clothes in Bron's room. The moment she silently cursed her sister for being a shopaholic, shampoo seeped into her paper cut. Touché, Libby, Bron thought, holding her pinkie directly under the showerhead to rinse away the sting.

The dress would have fit better a size smaller. Libby's shoulders had always been wider than hers, but Bron thought she could get away with it. Not wanting to trigger anything in Annie, she sprayed enough of her own perfume to disguise the scent of her sister which had seeped its way into the material during its close proximity to the other clothes on the rack.

When she made her way downstairs, Annie was seated at the kitchen table. Oddly, her oversized school bag was already on her back, wedging her closer to the plate of raisin toast in front of her.

Bron bent at the waist to kiss the top of Annie's perfect braid. "Your hair looks lovely, sweetheart. Did Nanna do that for you?"

Annie nodded, her mouth full of toast.

Across the table, Ally looked up from buttering her own raisin toast. "Morning," she said, the smile she offered Bron so bright it bared teeth. If it was my first morning out of prison, I'd probably be a morning person too, Bron thought. Politely, she smiled back.

"Sleep well?" Jackie asked from the end of the table.

Bron flicked on the kettle. "Fine."

"Hurry up, Annie," Daniel called from the back veranda. "I'll be in the ute waiting for the both of you."

Ally stood, a half-eaten slice of toast perched between her perfectly straight teeth. "C'mon, Goldilocks," Ally said. She picked up Annie's plate and dumped it in the sink.

Copying Ally, Annie struggled to grip her own leftover toast between her teeth, the slice almost as wide as her face.

"You're eager to get to school for once," Bron laughed, wiping a few crumbs off her cheek with her thumb.

"Ally's taking me!" Annie mumbled.

Squeezing Annie goodbye, Jackie grinned across the kitchen at Bron in bemusement as she followed her niece outside.

"Have you got your homework book?" she called after her, watching as Ally opened the back door for Annie.

"I think so," Annie called back, tossing the rest of her toast to Tammy, who gobbled it up in an instant.

"What about your spelling book?"

"I think so."

She leaned against a timber beam and crossed her arms. "You think so or you know so?"

Ally slammed the car door closed behind the little girl and Annie's reply was lost. Before she climbed into the passenger's seat, Ally nodded toward Bron. "See ya."

She was halfway down the steps when she stopped. Ally was already on it. Her upper body was bent over the console as she leaned into the back, pulling the black strap across Annie's lap to be sure Annie was buckled in, that Libby's baby girl was safe.

"Have a good day, Daniel!" Bron called as she watched her brother lock the tray of the ute. She threw a look toward the car, making sure Ally had the air on rather than the windows down. In a lower voice, she said just for Daniel's ears, "Keep an eye out for yourself today, too, Daniel. Okay?"

Knowing exactly what she was implying, he scowled. "Go get some work done for once, Bron!"

She waited until the ute rounded the corner at the end of the driveway and onto the street before she went back inside. Jackie had a cup of tea waiting for her. "That's a nice dress, love."

"Thanks." Bron scooped the crumbs from Annie's toast into her cupped hand and tossed them into the sink. "It was Libby's. Still had its tags," she added.

"Looks very nice on you, my girl."

Bron sipped at her tea and sighed. Jackie always made it perfectly.

"Wasn't that southerly heavenly this morning?"

She hummed her agreement as she sat down at the table. "Especially heavenly when I didn't have a restless six-year-old sweating the bed next to me."

"Yes," Jackie chuckled. "I heard on the grapevine that she's found a new best friend. She'll tire of Ally soon enough."

She scoffed. "I doubt she'd even notice if I left and went back home."

"Bron," Jackie grumbled. She smothered her toast in a thick layer of heart-smart butter, defeating the purpose. "Now that Ally's out of prison, it changes the dynamic. You've got to understand that Al is familiar. She's been a constant in Annie's life since she was born."

"A constant?" Bron would have been outraged by what she was hearing if it wasn't so laughable. "How can somebody be a constant from behind bars?"

"I'll tell you exactly how. Annie's spent every second Saturday morning in that horrible prison crèche since she was this high." Jackie reached her hand two feet above the kitchen floor. "She went out there and visited Ally every time Libby did. And, let me tell you, Ally has adored that girl since the day Libby forced Annie's itty-bitty body into her arms. For heaven's sake, we've got photos of Annie pretending to blow out the candles of her third birthday cake in the visitor centre because, for obvious reasons, they don't let you light candles in there."

Bron shook her head. "Prison is no place for a child. Even if it is just for visiting." She paused. "Didn't she ask questions?"

"Lots of questions. And Annie probably learned more about forgiveness and what it means to be a good person from her visits with Ally than she ever could have in a church."

Bron raised an eyebrow and got up from her seat. "Well, I never would have thought that a statement like that could come from Mother Theresa herself."

Jackie scowled playfully. "That reminds me, I need to visit St. Stephens after lunch and water the lilies. They'll be on their last legs with this heat. Can you drop me down there before your meeting?"

She nodded. Her lips twisted into a smirk as she filled the sink to wash the breakfast plates. The fact that the church had a newly installed, state-of-the-art air-conditioning system had not escaped her. Yes, her stepmother was *just* like Mother Theresa, if Mother Theresa had founded a missionary in The Hamptons.

After Bron dropped Jackie off outside the church and Jackie assured her she would get a lift home from Father Jeff, Bron drove on to the heart of Katoomba. With the window down, the warm breeze caught the end of her ponytail, the soft hairs whipping the top of her arm. Even for a Tuesday afternoon, the streets were relatively empty. There were a few backpackers smoking outside the youth hostel on the main street, but she only counted five people on the city-bound platform of Katoomba Station waiting for the four p.m. train. Saturday would be a different story, when all the tourists would swarm in to see The Three Sisters at the bottom of the hill.

She parked in the vacant lot beside Dougall's Meats and reached down for the handle to manually roll up the window.

She hoped the air-conditioning in the café was working. The last thing she felt like doing was drinking a steaming cappuccino in a sauna; however, it would go hand-in-hand with the discomfort of spending her afternoon making idle chitchat with Alice Wood.

After picking up her phone from the mobile repair store, she headed south on Main Street. Three stores away, she spotted Alice's lanky form seated at a small table at the front window of the café. Conveniently, Alice had taken it upon herself to take the one seat at the table that happened to be out of the sun's glare.

A chill hit Bron the moment she walked inside, and she sighed at the cool welcome of the air-conditioning. Alice looked up from the large portfolio in front of her. "Bron! Look at you. You're as tiny as you were in uni!"

As she clumsily hugged her old friend, she looked over Alice's shoulder at the myriad of empty tables. When they pulled away from each other, Alice gestured to the seat opposite, and began to sit back down again.

"Could we maybe sit at the back?" Bron asked, gesturing to a pair of lounge chairs in the corner of the room, directly beneath the air conditioner. "The sun is blinding me here."

"Oh," Alice gasped, her tone poorly imitating sudden realisation. She looked around, as though the room was completely occupied and she was searching for a free seat. "It's just that I'm all set up here. Did you forget your sunglasses? Would you like to borrow mine?"

She waved her hand dismissively and pulled out a chair, immediately feeling the heat radiating from the glass and onto her bare shoulder. She should have listened to herself last week before mailing Alice the sketches—when she almost had herself convinced that getting professionally involved with Alice again was a stupid idea.

"How are your kids?" she dutifully asked.

"They're good. Skye is at uni down in Melbourne studying engineering, and Nate's finishing high school next year."

"Wow, you have a kid in uni." She shook her head. "That's insane."

Alice grinned widely but her features softened after a moment. "I'm very, very sorry to hear about your sister."

She swallowed. "Thank you." Under Alice's intense, sympathetic gaze, she chewed at the inside of her lip. "How's the city treating you?"

"Hotter than up here." Alice clasped her hands over the cover of Bron's portfolio. "Bron, these sketches are fantastic. Not at all what I remember your style to be or what I've seen you do recently."

"You've been following my work?"

"Well, it's hard not to when you illustrate basically every piece of children's literature under the sun." Alice grinned. "I'm very happy for you."

She smiled at the compliment. "Thanks, Alice. It didn't happen overnight, but it—"

"Honestly," Alice interrupted, "I think you should just give up Yellowstone and come and work for me instead."

It was what Bron had feared. She was willing to work with Alice on one project, just to keep Alice in her contact book if she ever needed a job in the future. But she doubted she could handle more of Alice than a single project required. Alice was too...frank. If Bron was going to give up Yellowstone for anything, it was going to be for MIT. She couldn't help but wonder how Alice would react to the news that a position was waiting for Bron in the art history department of one of the world's most prestigious universities. Teaching was a career change Bron had dreamed about for years. For the past six years, she'd submitted application after application to the Ivy Leagues, and each application had received the same response—her body of published work was outstanding, her postgraduate studies highly impressive, but there weren't any positions available. Until now. Bron had desperately wanted to share the news with somebody since she'd received the call the day before Ally arrived home, but she was well aware that her overwhelming joy would only serve to upset her family. Now her happiness was a dirty little secret that weighed heavily on her mind each night as she laid down to sleep. She only had until January to decide what the hell she was going to do. Could she actually see herself picking up the phone and turning down her alma mater in a few months' time when January rolled around? It would destroy that hopeful part of her that was only just beginning to slowly claw its way back home.

She took in Alice. Clearly, she hadn't changed much since university. She was still driven, as ambitious as ever. While Bron had taken off to the States to finish graduate school studying art history at MIT, Alice had decided against graduate school and had immediately found work as an intern with one of the leading publishers in Australia. She'd been climbing the editorial ladder ever since. By the time Bron had graduated and was in the early days of establishing a freelance career, Alice was married with a newborn baby. It had become an unspoken, mutual acknowledgment that their friendship had fizzled into nothing more than professional contacts.

"Well, I can't exactly throw in the bag with Yellowstone," she started, "but my contract stipulates that I can work on up to four independent projects annually for other publishers."

Alice gestured to the barista, blatantly ignoring Bron's offer. Bron twisted in her seat and looked toward the counter. As far as she knew, the café had never offered table service. She gathered from the struggle burning darkly in the barista's eyes as he crossed the room toward them that the café was in fact *not* table service.

"A tall, decaf latte—wait, you do decaf, of course?" Alice prompted.

He nodded curtly and looked to Bron.

"Could I please have a small cappuccino?" She added a wide smile, hoping it smoothed over Alice's rudeness.

When he left, Alice looked down at the sketches. "Bron, I'm senior editor now, and that gives me a great deal of authority in selecting illustrators to be matched with our picture book authors." She paused, offering a serious stare. "I'm willing to go above what Yellowstone is paying."

Bron forced a smile, hating the way her hands trembled beneath the table, hating that this woman—who was nothing more than her equal—could intimidate her. "To be honest, Alice, I don't know if we work well together." When Alice's eyes grew large, Bron placated. "I don't know if we're a good match. We both have very strong opinions. Don't you remember how we clashed working on uni projects together?"

"Look," Alice interrupted, waving her worries away with a manicured hand. "You can't say no to me. I've already got an author lined up for you."

She was grateful when the barista brought over their coffees and she had a second to get her wits about her. How had her twenty-year-old self managed to spend five afternoons a week commuting all the way to and from Sydney Uni alone on a train with this woman?

"When are you going back to Boston?" Alice prompted, her tone dripping with the insinuation that she already had it all figured out for her.

Bron shifted and unstuck her thighs from the wooden seat. "A month or so."

"So how about I send you the narrative and you draw up a few drafts for me before then?"

The commanding question immediately put her offside, but the promise of a higher advance was tempting. She was able to live more than comfortably on her current salary, but she had Annie to think of now—school fees, health insurance, a university fund, the cost of raising a child. With Libby gone, that responsibility fell to Bron, and she was more than happy to assume it.

"I have another idea."

Alice lifted an eyebrow. "Which is?"

"I give this author you have lined up for me a miss and I start working for you when I come back to Australia—*if* I don't decide to continue with Yellowstone."

"You're moving back here?" Alice inquired.

"Perhaps. I have sole custody of Annie." She drew a breath, inching farther away from the glass. "I'll be going back to sort out a few things with Yellowstone, but when I return...who knows? All I'm certain of is that I need to be where Annie is or she needs to be with me." *And that may very well be in Boston with me.*

"What about the girl's father?"

"He's in Queensland." She decided it was best not to go into detail about Annie's paternal woes with Alice. "She doesn't know him."

Alice's bright red painted lips twisted. "Coming back makes sense. Besides, it's not like you've got your own family to look after over there." Bron blinked twice, offended by Alice's bluntness. "Hey, it works for me if you come back," Alice continued. "Are you absolutely sure you can't start with this author?"

As the afternoon sun drooped, Bron refused Alice's offer three more times. Rejecting her persistent friend was more exhausting than having to endure a slideshow presentation of what seemed like Alice's kids' entire childhood. Surely the phone memory would reach capacity at some point, Bron thought as the images scrolled past on the small screen.

After Alice refrained from pulling out her wallet when they got up to leave, Bron paid the bill and made for the car park just as her phone rang. She looked down at the caller ID and grinned.

"Aunt Bron, where are ya?" Annie asked.

She wedged her phone between her ear and shoulder as she started the car. "I'm in town. I'm heading home now."

"Nanna says we're gonna have a barbie, so can ya pick up some bread rolls?"

She looked down at her watch. "Honey, it's going to close in five minutes. Is Ally home? Maybe she can run down to the end of the street with you and pick them up?"

"Nah, she's not home yet," Annie said distractedly. Jackie's voice was muffled in the background. "Nan says can you just try?"

The bakery at the end of her street was almost closed by the time Bron pulled up in front of the tiny mud-brick store. As she slid the glass door of the bakery open, the nostalgic scent of freshly baked bread assaulted her senses.

"Hi, Lars," she called to her first employer. He stopped sweeping the racks over with a hand brush—just as Bron could recall her teenage self doing—and turned toward the door. "Long time no see."

"Bronwyn Lee!" He folded his arms on the metal rack. "How've you been? Real sorry to hear about your sister. She was such a lovely thing."

She smiled softly. "Thanks, Lars." She looked down at the trays of bread rolls she knew Lars would soon tally as wastage. "I saw your Jan a few weeks ago. She's looking well."

"She mentioned it, darl. How's the States working out for you? Did you land yourself a fella over there for a green card?"

Here we go again, Bron thought. "No husband. I'm gay. But I'm not one to marry for a green card anyway, so I had to go through the work channels for the visa."

Elderly Lars was clearly at a loss for words, but he quickly recovered from the shock of her reveal. "Well, each to their own, love. There's nothing wrong with that! I knew a gay back in school and he was a top bloke, real top bloke..."

Thanks for your approval, she thought sardonically, but Lars was old, so she let it go. "Have any hot dog rolls left?" she asked.

With a bag full of free hot dog rolls and a special treat for Annie for later, she drove up the hill, surprised to find the driveway gates were open. A brief wave of panic swept over her at the possibility that Tammy had gotten out, but as she drew closer to the house, she spotted Daniel's ute and her heart rate slowed.

"I'm home," she called as she unlocked the front door.

"We're out here," Daniel replied. She could smell sausages wafting from around the side of the house.

"Is Tams with you?" she asked as she dropped her keys on the kitchen table.

"Yep."

She headed out the back through the laundry, but stopped when she found Ally and Annie bent over the deep washtub. Ally stood in a puddle of water in her dirtied work boots. The pair of old work shorts she wore—which had seemed decent on Libby—were almost *too* short on Ally's longer legs. Dirty, dusty, *toned* legs. When she forced herself to look up, Ally's gaze was on her, observing her calculated stare. Ally smirked and Bron looked away.

Ally adjusted her hold on Annie, lifting her higher to the sink. Propped on Ally's hip, Annie giggled as Ally bent over the tub and soaped her hands. She scrubbed all the way up Annie's arms and created a soapy mess, which earned a loud cackle from Annie as water ran down both their elbows, saturating Jackie's tiled laundry floor.

"Gosh, Annie, are they teaching you to make mud pies at school or what?" Ally mumbled.

"The dirt ain't coming from my hands. It's your dirt!" Annie argued.

Ally's laughter was deep and genuine.

When Bron came closer with a handtowel and into her niece's line of sight, Annie's eyebrows shot up. "You're home, Aunt Bron! You gonna wash up too?" Annie's eyes fell to the wrapped iced tea bun in her hand. She squealed and wiggled down from Ally's grip.

"Pink icing! Yes!" She pumped her fist into the air, running forward and grabbing for the bag of bread.

Bron pulled back and set the plastic bag down on the lid of the washing machine. "No tea bun until after dinner, missy. Dry your hands and then take the bread rolls outside to Nan. How was school?"

Annie took the handtowel from Bron. "It was okay. Ally and Dan picked me up."

As Annie made her quick escape outside, she smiled at Ally, who was vigorously scrubbing her forearms. Ally smiled back. Bron reached for the bottle of hand soap and squirted a coin-sized amount onto her palm. The words Ally muttered were too soft over the running water.

"I missed that?" Bron said.

Ally cleared her throat. "I said, 'nice dress.'"

Almost on cue, the soap Bron was rubbing into her skin soaked into the paper cut, reopening the wound. The damn dress was cursed. Bron wet her lips. "Thank you." She tried to ignore the bloodless sting. "It must have been a hot day outside for you and Daniel," she tried. "I wasn't exactly doing hard labour and even I'm perspiring."

Ally's lips twisted into a grin. She looked Bron up and down. "Doesn't look like it."

Suddenly, Ally bent forward and stuck her whole head beneath the tap, saturating her short hair. Water ran down the curve of her neck, drenching the razor back of her navy singlet. Bron forced her gaze away from Ally's firm, tanned breasts spilling over the rim of her singlet. She couldn't help but notice the skin surrounding the tattoo, violently red the day before, was now just irritated pink.

Ally pulled back from the tub. Slicking a hand through her hair, she looked around for a towel. Bron offered her the handtowel to wipe at the water raining from her chin, but Ally reached behind her to the washing basket, full of fresh linens from the clothes line. She snatched up the pale blue towel with the embroidered 'B.'

"Oh—"

"Let me guess. This one's not okay?" Ally sighed.

Bron looked up and met Ally's stare. No, she hadn't imagined the bite in Ally's tone.

Ally cocked an eyebrow. She looked…completely drained.

It wasn't worth the argument. "No, I…it's fine. Totally fine."

Ally leaned back against the linen cupboard, rubbing at her wet hair, her jawline, her arms, all with Bron's towel. She gestured toward the running tap. "Are you going to wash those hands sometime today?" she wondered, the scrape of her voice gravelly.

Right, hands. Soapy water.

"Excuse me," she mumbled, widening her legs over the puddle at the base of the sink.

Ally pulled the towel over her neck and disappeared out the back door.

Five seconds was all it took. "Hey, that's Aunty Bron's towel!" Annie immediately chided. Bron closed her eyes and cringed. "She doesn't let anyone use her towel!" Annie continued. "You better put it back before she sees."

Ally knew Bron was within earshot. She had to say something. "That's okay! Don't worry about it," she called, but Ally's work boots were already climbing up the back steps.

Bron licked her lips and turned off the tap as the back screen creaked open.

"Really, it doesn't matter," Bron began.

"I think this belongs to you." Ally deposited the towel in Bron's wet hands. "Wouldn't want to get in your bad book again," she said, making for the door.

Bron pressed against the tub. "What makes you think you're in my bad book?" she asked. Even the *way* Ally said it sounded too polite, too contrived.

When Ally met her gaze, it was obvious Ally believed she'd never been in Bron's good book. Ally hesitated at the door for a moment before she crossed the room and stepped directly in front of Bron, so close she could feel her body heat. Unsure of Ally's reaction, she was unmoving. She dropped her gaze to the floor, and watched out the corner of her eye as Ally's fingers curled tightly around the lip of the tub.

Ally craned her neck slightly so her words were for Bron's ears only. "Here's the thing: I don't care if you like me, Bron," she whispered. "You don't have to like me, and you don't have to trust me. I know you think I'm no good because I owe you a shitload of money and I fucked with Libby's life. But this family's all I've got, and I know they'd like it if we got along."

Bron raised her gaze from the sink. In weariness, Ally's eyes, usually the colour of a fine cognac, were lighter. It was the setting sun streaming through the window, Bron realized, which set golden rays flickering in Ally's irises.

A deep sigh fell from Ally's lips. "So how about we just call it a day and be done with it?"

She searched her face for any hint of insincerity, but only found frustration in her expression. "Don't look at me like that," Bron asserted.

Ally was infuriatingly calm. "Like what?"

"Like *that*. The way we look at Annie when she's pushed it too far. Like I'm at fault."

"This," Ally said, waving a hand between them, "is exactly what I'm talking about. I'm ready to be done with it. Are you?"

Bron was ready to be done with *the conversation*. Dropping the towel on top of the full load in the washing machine, she nodded.

"That's a yes?" Ally encouraged, searching Bron's face for confirmation.

"Yes."

"Okay." Ally clicked her tongue. She paused, unmoving. "Is there anything you want to say to me?"

"Nope." The intensity of Ally's stare bore hotly into the side of Bron's cheek as she turned the dials on the machine.

"Good," Ally said, pushing off the tub and heading back outside.

Bron drew a deep breath. She could forgive for Annie's sake, for her family's sake. But she wouldn't forget.

CHAPTER FOUR

Holding the garden hose loosely in one hand, Bron watched Daniel scrape charcoal from the barbecue grill plate. At her feet, Annie splashed around in the shallow kiddie pool Bron was filling with cooler water, mumbling mindlessly as she constructed an imaginary rainforest world with Jackie's water can and Libby's old Safari Barbie. Bron appraised her brother, so charming in his sophisticated button-up and his pale grey dressy shorts. She thought about just how serious his relationship with Carly Jamieson actually was.

Carly's parents had timed their overseas cruise to arrive in Sydney Harbour that Friday morning, the morning of Carly's twenty-first birthday. But an upset Carly had arrived on their doorstep the night before, after her parents had called with the unfortunate news that, due to poor weather conditions that day, the ship was behind schedule. The Jamiesons wouldn't be back in Katoomba until the early hours of Saturday morning. Daniel suggested Carly reschedule the extended family dinner to Saturday night, when her parents were back in the mountains.

On the night of her birthday, he'd cook for her. From the lounge in the front room, Bron had watched Carly's fallen expression transform into one of elation.

She watched Daniel count out the marinated steaks and tip a prepackaged bag of lettuce into one of Jackie's salad bowls that had been around since the eighties. She had to give him credit for effort. Although she felt underdressed in her shorts and singlet, she imagined if there was going to be an award for the *Most Disappointing Aspect of Carly Jamieson's Twenty-First Birthday Dinner*, it probably wasn't going to be her outfit.

As Daniel crouched down and checked the gas bottle, Bron raised her Aviators to the top of her head. "You know they've called out a total fire ban?"

He scoffed, his focus trained on lighting the barbecue. "Yes, Bronwyn, I am familiar with the NSW Rural Fire Service Rules and Regulations."

She squinted in the sun. "Well, isn't it a better idea to cook those inside?"

"Excuse me, Miss High and Mighty, it's gas-fired. Besides, am I lighting it for cooking, or for comfort and warmth?"

She wiped at her clammy forehead. "Definitely not comfort and warmth." Even after five thirty, it seemed the burning sun had no intention of ever setting. As it was, the wading pool was more like a spa bath. She was surprised the cheap plastic hadn't melted flat into the grass beneath.

Annie twisted on the plastic mat of the pool lightly splashing Bron's shorts and the minute patch of skin where her navel was exposed.

"Why are you complaining?" he played. "Don't you want barbecued octopus?"

"As we're all well aware, this family doesn't have the best reputation when it comes to following RFS laws," she said casually, flicking her wrist and allowing a thin fountain of warm water to drizzle over Annie's hair. "*Especially* former firewomen."

He ripped open a packet of sausages with a sharp knife. "Can you just let it go?"

"I have let it go," she retorted.

"When are Nanna and Ally coming back with the seeing food?" Annie interrupted.

"Seafood," he corrected. "Soon. Ann, how about you go get dried off and put on the new dress Carly gave you for your birthday?"

Annie reclined in the pool and shook her head. "It itches."

"Well," he continued, "I'm sure Carly would really like to see you in it."

Annie sighed deeply. "Okay."

When Annie was out of earshot, he turned to Bron. "You know why Ally lit up his garage, right?"

Bron raised an eyebrow and nodded. She knew he was referring to Annie's father and Libby's ex.

He shook his head. "Then I don't understand why you can't be a little bit more sympathetic. He wasn't a good guy, Bron. He wasn't good to Libby or Annie."

She dropped the hose and turned it off. "I *know* that, but Ally could have killed him. And you know how she got when she didn't have Libby's undivided attention."

"It wasn't like that."

"You were barely seventeen, Dan. You don't know the half of it—"

"I know *all* of it. She wasn't trying to kill him. The garage was twenty metres from the house. Besides," he raised a hand, knowing exactly what Bron was going to protest, "she knew he wasn't home. The only life she intended on taking that night was that of his Mercedes, and she did a bloody good job of it, let me tell you."

Bron blinked twice. "How do you know?"

He shrugged. "My friend Matty and I rode over there the next night—"

"You're an idiot!"

"Relax. He wasn't even home. We only went into the garage, saw the car and took off."

Bron was curious. "How badly burnt out was it?"

"Well, she called the RFS like two minutes after setting it alight, so it wasn't that bad. There mustn't have been much fuel in the car or maybe she emptied it first. I don't know. But the roof had caved in, and the car was scorched like it had been to hell and back. You just can't make this shit up."

She blew at a few loose strands of hair. "That's ridiculous. What I can't get over—I couldn't even believe it when Lib told me—was that she called the RFS. Why do it in the first place if you're just going to dob yourself in?"

"She was being responsible."

Bron couldn't help but laugh. "Responsible?"

Daniel couldn't find the humour in it. It amazed her how completely Ally had their family wrapped around her little finger. "Look, say what you want, but she knew how to play with fire, Bron. She knew how to start it, maintain it, and when it was time, put it out before it spread. And before you go and put your foot in it like you did with the money she owes you, it wasn't calling the RFS that dobbed her in—it was her mum."

Bron couldn't hide her shock. She hadn't known that. "Ally's mum told the police?"

He nodded. "She told them Al hadn't been home and she'd seen her take off in the truck around eleven that night with what looked like a bag—the fuel. The old bitch's statement fit with Al's boot prints outside his house and the security tape of her filling up a fuel container outside Leura a few days before."

"Yeah," Bron said quietly. "I knew about the print and the fuel container. I just didn't know about her mother."

He looked toward the house and then down at his sister. "I think he used to hit Libby," he said, his voice thick with solemnity.

The thought choked her hard. "What?"

His jaw clenched. "I mean I never saw her with a black eye or anything, but I'm pretty sure he did something. I think Ally found out after Libby left him to come and live with us. That's why she went over there and went all firestarter on his ass."

She shook her head. "No. Libby would have said something to me."

He shrugged. "Maybe she told Ally instead."

It wasn't as though dark thoughts of Libby's ex hadn't crossed her mind before. After Annie's birth, he'd become a full-fledged jerk. But she was certain that if domestic violence had been the case, Libby would have confided in her. *Wouldn't she?* Even if oceans had separated them, the sisters had always been incredibly close. But Daniel's suggestion was not out of the question. She looked down at the raw steaks swimming in soy sauce and felt like she was going to throw up.

He cleared his throat. "If I had known back then, I swear I would have done something myself." She looked up at his face, his expression etched with too much severity and frustration for a twenty-three-year-old. "But I didn't realize until much later."

She pressed a hand between his shoulder blades and rubbed his back. "Well, I'm glad you didn't because you're too damn pretty to go to prison."

He chuckled as he always did when the mood became too serious. "Don't try to school me," he said, but Bron was too consumed by thoughts of how lucky they all were to have Daniel—especially Annie. "Your American accent is showing," he added. She was about to banter before a flash of red—her old car—stopped at the end of the driveway and caught her attention. In front of the car, the postman rode past on his motorbike, lifting a hand to thank Ally and Jackie for stopping.

Panic instantly flushed through Bron, breaking over her in a sweat the very second she remembered the drafts for her upcoming deadline. Barefoot, she jumped up the back steps, the screen door swinging behind her. She bounded upstairs, the sound of Daniel calling after her carrying through the house. "The postie!" she shouted back.

In a mad rush, she swept the drafts off her bedroom desk. *Where was the bloody Express Post envelope?* Her heart hammering, she quickly glanced up from the pile of papers strewn across the desk and out the window. Through the trees and bushes, she could see the postbox outside the bakery at the bottom of the street and the postman's fluorescent orange vest as he pulled up to it.

"Shit, shit, shit," she muttered, scanning the room until she found the plastic yellow envelope beneath her bed.

She took the stairs two at a time. Jackie had the boot of the car open and was in the process of unloading groceries when Bron ran out the front door. "Quick, chuck me the keys. I'm going to miss him!"

Jackie's eyes fell to the papers, pen and envelope Bron held. Understanding quickly rained on her. "Ally's around the side. She's got the keys. Love, he'll already be at the box…"

Just as the hot, dry breeze caught the top paper in her arms and carried it across the front lawn, Ally came from around the side, the car keys jingling from her fingers.

"I need the keys!" Bron exclaimed, bending down to chase the page.

Ally grabbed it and handed it to her. "Come on, I'll drive you." Before she could protest that Ally's licence was expired, Ally added, "You still need to address the bag and it's just to the end of the street."

As Ally turned the car around, Bron shoved the drafts into the envelope and scribbled down the publisher's address. She sealed it, her heart racing. "I cannot believe I forgot."

Ally looked down at the envelope. "Work?"

"Drafts for a new book. They need to be in Sydney by Monday."

"You can't just scan and email them?"

She shook her head, concentrating more on getting ready to jump out to open the front gate than Ally's questions. "Scanners don't pick up fine detail."

"Well, I've got all night to drive into the city if we miss him."

"You have until exactly ten o'clock."

Ally pulled the car to a rough stop. "I'll get the gate," she said and pointed to the bag. "You've forgotten to fill in the sender's address."

Bron groaned and picked up the pen again. By the time they turned into the street, Bron could see the postman was gone. She sighed deeply. "Which way do you think he went?"

Ally made a left onto Eveleigh Street. Her gaze fell to Bron's bare, bouncing knee. "Relax, we'll catch him."

Bron looked out the back window and surveyed the cross streets for the postman. When they turned onto the main street of Katoomba and passed the café where she'd had her meeting earlier that week, she told Ally to pull over.

"Come on, what are the chances of getting caught? Besides, you haven't even got your licence with you."

She huffed, deeply irritated. It was worse than arguing with Annie. "Just pull over, okay?"

Reluctantly Ally groaned and flicked the blinker to pull into a space. Her jaw seemed to tighten with frustration at being told what to do. Bron had never seen such an attractive scowl. She could *almost* be attracted to this woman—purely on a physical level, of course—if Ally didn't behave like a petulant child ninety percent of the time.

As if on cue, Ally cut the engine completely just for added effect, but Bron refused to bite. They got out and swapped sides, their arms colliding as they passed in front of the bonnet. She started the engine, listening desperately as it kicked over twice and finally grabbed. She didn't doubt for a second that the car's hesitancy to kick over would have brought Ally great pleasure, but she wouldn't give her the satisfaction of a glare.

Ally reached forward and turned up the volume of the radio. Bron barely allowed a line of "Piano Man" before she reached forward and spun the dial to mute. "Please, Ally! I'm trying to picture where another Express Postbox is, and you're making it very hard for me to think."

Ally scoffed and slid down in the passenger seat. She looked out the window as Bron zipped through town on a postman-stalking expedition. They found him emptying a postbox in a back street behind the train station. She wasn't oblivious to just how ridiculous she looked, swerving into a stranger's driveway, jumping out of the car barefoot and breathlessly explaining how she'd driven all the way from Maple Street to catch him. She barely coaxed a smile from him when she finished her tale, but when she turned back to the car, she could see Ally's amused expression.

Bron slumped into the driver's seat and breathed a deep sigh of relief. Her bare feet burned from the blistering pavement of the footpath. She pulled at her hair tie and gathered her long hair into a neater bun. "That was really close," she muttered.

"You've even got an audience," Ally noted.

Bron looked up. An elderly couple were standing with their front door wide open, surveying who had pulled into their driveway. They were a pair. Each had a hand on a hip, while the other served as a visor against the descending sun. They squinted across their front lawn at the running car.

Bron smirked. "Stickybeaks."

They drove back in silence until she recalled her mood minutes earlier. "Sorry about the radio. I was really stressed."

"No biggie," Ally said.

She was surprised, even impressed, when a few seconds passed and Ally hadn't added anything else like a snarky comment.

Bron cleared her throat. "Thanks, Al."

"No worries. Besides," she said, looking out of the passenger window, "you've always been a drama queen and a half."

By the time they returned, Carly's car was in the driveway. The family was seated around the backyard table, which Jackie had set with the good china. The barbecue sizzled with the fresh seafood Jackie and Ally had picked up earlier, and if it weren't for the missing lobster rolls, Bron could almost pretend she was back in Boston.

She was the first to hug Carly and wish her a happy birthday. Ally stood back and smiled awkwardly as Bron apologised for their lateness and then introduced Ally.

"Catch him?" Jackie asked as she came down the steps with a cheese platter in hand.

"Catch who?" Carly wondered as she poured Bron and Ally drinks.

"Bron's lusting after the postie," Ally said seriously.

Annie popped a cube of cheese into her mouth. "What's 'lusting' mean?"

Bron blushed and shook her head. "Never mind."

Carly looked confused. "Ally, do you drink Moscato?" she offered, the lip of the wine bottle hovering over a clean glass.

Bron looked up, wondering just how far Ally thought that she could push it.

"I drink anything with alcohol," she said. Bron didn't miss the second when Ally's stare very briefly flickered toward her. "But unfortunately, I'll have to say no. You know, the whole parole thing." She waved her hand, casting her extensive criminal history aside as yesterday's news.

"Oh," Carly said, her cheeks reddening. "I didn't know you were out on parole. I thought—"

Ally bit into a cracker and cheese. "Hey, no skin off my nose. It's nice for someone to give me a break once in a while," she said pointedly, and Bron knew it was said for her ears.

When dinner was ready and idle chitchat over drinks ended, Bron found herself seated at the back table next to a prettily-dressed Annie, who eagerly encouraged Ally to sit on her other side. But it wasn't long before Annie was sighing that she was full and was excused from the table. Had Bron imagined the way Ally shifted closer to her when Annie got up to play with Tammy?

"So…law school," Ally said as she cut into her steak. Bron looked down between them and watched the way the tendons in Ally's forearm tensed as she sliced the overcooked meat. "That sounds like a handful."

Carly swallowed and wiped at her lips with a napkin. "Well, the semester's almost over, but I'm hoping to take up an internship before the year's end."

"Oh, really?" Ally asked. "Where?"

"There's a great program running through the legal aid office. One of my professors has a contact to set me up with, so I'm hoping that it will work out."

"She's gonna get it," Daniel guaranteed. "She's going to make a damn good lawyer sometime soon."

Ally drizzled balsamic dressing over the salad on her plate. "Legal aid's good when they're good."

Carly raised an eyebrow. "You had a legal aid lawyer?"

"Three," Ally said. "I got rid of the first two for incompetence," she added.

Bron's head shot up, ready to laugh at the idea of Ally having had the hide to be picky, but it seemed as though everyone else had missed the memo. Ally must have noticed, because she added, "I may have torched a car but I still had my rights."

"So are you planning on working with Daniel into the new year?" Carly asked. "I know he's loved having you around. He comes over every night so relaxed. Don't you?" she asked Daniel, playing with the hair at the nape of his neck.

Bron lifted her leg over the seat to get another prawn kebab from the barbecue. Ally shifted for her, but their thighs still pressed together. However fleeting the touch was, their gazes locked awkwardly for a second until Bron removed herself completely from the seat.

"Well, Carly, I've been told I have a woman's touch," Ally joked. "But not exactly anything you've got to worry about."

When Bron heard Carly laugh, she knew Ally's face was lit up with a cocky grin. A thought came to her, and instantly, strangely, made her feel uneasy. Ally must have been popular in prison.

All night, Bron wanted—needed—to catch Ally alone. She had to know about Libby. She found Ally on the veranda, chewing on a leftover prawn kebab from dinner.

"Did you have a good night?" Bron asked, leaning against a veranda post.

Ally smiled at her from the swing chair. "Yeah, it was nice to be rewarded with a decent meal after a hard week's work for the first time in…five years."

She grinned. "What's Daniel like to work with?"

"Work *with*?" Ally raised an eyebrow. "You don't work with Daniel. You work *for* him." Bron chuckled, encouraging her to tell more. "He's really good. He lets me do my own thing. He listens. Doesn't hurt that he pays well too," she trailed off, her grin splitting at the growing smile she'd put on Bron's face.

"She's pretty cute," Ally said, pointing to Carly.

Bron turned and looked across the circular driveway to where Daniel and Carly were kissing Jackie good-bye, ready to head over to Carly's quiet and *empty* house for the night.

Ally pressed, "You don't think she's cute?"

She shrugged. "I think she's Daniel's girlfriend."

"That doesn't mean you can't pass on a few words of encouragement to him." Ally laughed. "He *does* know you're a dyke."

She crossed the veranda and sat down next to her. "Yes, but maybe they don't enjoy being reminded."

As she sat back, the swing started to rock slightly, and Ally raised a foot to the side table in front of them to stop the motion. "They don't care that you're gay, Bron. They don't care that either of us are."

She sighed. "It can be easy to mistake tolerance for support."

Ally pushed against the table, the swing subtly rocking. "You're pretty bitter," she said softly.

Either the scent of the bougainvillea that leeched its way from around the side to the front veranda or the controlled rocking of the swing—or both—calmed her. "Can I ask you something?"

Ally threw the wooden kebab stick down onto the table and nodded.

Bron faced her. "Why did you torch his garage?"

Ally stilled her foot against the table, the swing ceasing its movement. "Because he was a mongrel."

Bron looked at her intently. "What happened?"

"What is it that you're wanting to know?"

"Did he ever hit Libby?"

Ally's expression slipped into sorrow. "Honestly...I don't know."

"So you just did it because you were angry?"

Ally grimaced. "He didn't realize how good he had it with Libby." It was clear to Bron that Ally was very carefully considering her next words. "She was different after she married him. You weren't here to see it, but she was...she was just *so sad*."

Bron felt the onslaught of tears, strong and fast. Suddenly it seemed very important that Ally didn't see her cry. She stood abruptly.

Ally sat forward, her arm dangling in midair, like a marionette without its puppeteer. "Are you okay?"

"Yeah, yeah," Bron assured her, but she wouldn't meet Ally's worried gaze. "I think I'll head to bed," she whispered in a voice that wasn't her own.

"Hey," Ally called after her.

Bron stopped at the front door.

"Mind if we go for that drive on Sunday?"

CHAPTER FIVE

Bron watched Ally through the rear vision mirror. She stood at the roadside flower canteen outside the cemetery gates, shifting from foot to foot in her dirtied work boots as she contemplated her options. She bent over what Bron assumed to be bunches of carnations—cheap, funeral flowers. She cringed. Ally stood up, placed a hand on her hip and rubbed her chin in frustration. Her lips moved in apology as she stepped aside for two elderly women picking matching bundles of roses.

It was Sunday morning after church, and there were more customers at the flower stall than usual. A part of Bron wanted to get out and help Ally, to guide her toward gerberas or lilies, or even a modest bunch of stock for Libby. Ally wouldn't know a rose from a weed. But Ally Shepherd had said that she would buy the flowers herself, and Bron wanted her to have at least that.

On the short drive to the cemetery in the next suburb over, it had been impossible to avoid Gibson Street, the connecting road to the highway. Unbeknownst to Ally, they had passed the telegraph pole Libby's car had wrapped itself around in a fatal embrace. Bron had silently encouraged herself to focus on the double white lines in the middle of the road. But seconds after they'd passed it, she'd looked into the rear vision mirror, spotting the wilting bunch of flowers strapped to the pole on the other side of the road, the yellow plastic wrapping as bright as Annie's school uniform. She'd refocused on her driving and pushed the thought of an unconscious, trapped Annie to the back of her mind, permitting the haunting thought to return later that day if it would simply leave her alone for *now*, so that she could just get through *this*.

Ally moved to the counter, her arms full with at least three bunches. How nice, Bron thought. She knew Ally made just ten cents an hour from her kitchen detail in prison and had very little savings to her name. She'd only been working with Daniel for a week. It was admirable that she would spend so much on flowers for Libby.

She made her way back toward the car, her hands so full Bron reached over and flicked the passenger door open. When Ally climbed in, she made an unintelligible noise of uncertainty.

"No, they're lovely." Bron leaned over and put her nose to the bouquet of white roses. She smiled for Ally. "You chose wisely."

"I don't really know what this stuff is," Ally mumbled, nodding down to the baby's breath in her lap, "but I thought it'd go good with the white. It's not weird to buy roses for a grave, is it? I know she likes roses..." Ally rambled on, her use of the present tense not escaping Bron.

Bron cleared her throat and started the car. "White roses typically signify reverence. Or heavenliness."

Pleased, Ally nodded. She quietly sat back, the wrapped stems gripped tightly in her fist.

Bron drove to the back of the cemetery. They passed the war graves, which she hadn't noticed looking so dilapidated the last time she'd been here for Libby's burial. In fact, she hadn't noticed them at all. Some were almost on a sixty-degree lean into the next, like dominoes, as though, even in death, their namesakes still shared a sense of camaraderie. She drew to a stop when they reached the newer rows where the grass grew greener and wilder.

When Bron got out of the car, her feet were so heavy she could have sworn she was wearing lead boots rather than flimsy thongs. She led Ally halfway down the third row to the thigh-high white cross Daniel had made out of plywood and spray-painted. In his usually messy scrawl were perfect block letters: ELIZABETH LEE. No dates. It would have to do while they waited for the headstone to return from the stonemason.

Ally stood back, looking down at the cross, glancing up at the sky, returning her attention to the white plywood marker. For a long moment, they both fell silent.

"It's sunken again," Bron finally said.

"Yeah. You were right. It doesn't look too nice."

Ally stepped around the perimeter and laid out the bouquets of white roses and baby's breath.

"Would you like help?" Bron asked as Ally unwrapped the bunches.

"No, I've got it," she said, pulling the dehydrated, browning stems from the vase. Ally cut off the bases and checked their height against the vase. Bron felt like a stranger at a row of graves which, until Libby's passing, she'd been visiting since her mother died.

Ally unscrewed the vase from where its base was fixed to the concrete slab behind the cross. She stood and looked around. "Is there a tap where I can clean this out?"

Bron motioned to the end of the row. Ally walked off and Bron admired her tan, which was darker than when she'd first arrived. Her work shorts had given her an additional tan line too. There was a distinct border between olive and coffee-tinted skin on the back of her toned legs, especially obvious in the much shorter shorts she'd chosen that morning.

Bron looked across the road at the UGG boot stall, which had been running for as long as she could remember. Her first pair of pink UGGS was from there, way back in the nineties when wearing UGGS in public had been socially acceptable.

She cringed as she took in the giant cow skins hanging proudly around the shop, marking its perimeter. As off-putting as the visual was to her, tourists on their way to and from Sydney always stopped to land a good bargain, never finding any qualms with the animal cruelty on display *or* parking their rental cars in the cemetery. There's a time for everything, she thought. A time to be born, a time to die, a time for mourning, and a time for half-price genuine Aussie UGGS.

When Ally came back with the vase full of fresh water, she arranged the roses and their garnish with a kind of care and reverence Bron hadn't thought she possessed.

Ally stood back to admire her handiwork. "Looks okay, right?"

Knowing her voice would falter, Bron simply nodded her approval. She should have let Jackie bring Ally.

Ally didn't try to talk at the plywood cross as though it were Libby, like Annie said Jackie did. Perhaps, like Bron, Ally felt there wasn't any point. There was no real motivation for Bron's life-long atheism other than simple scepticism. She tried to put herself in Ally's shoes. She'd been imprisoned for five years for protecting her best friend, only for Libby to die just months before she was granted parole? If there was a higher power, it had certainly played a cruel joke on her.

Ally gathered the plastic and paper wrapping from the flowers and nervously moulded them into a ball in her hands. "So...You said that your parents are here?"

Bron pointed to the plot next to Libby's: *Margaret Lee.* "That's my father's mother." It was a much older, decrepit headstone. Their father had tried to refurbish it years before he died, but now the lettering was flaking again. The first three letters were barely legible. If anybody came looking for the late Garet Lee of Leura, they'd have less trouble finding him than someone looking for Nanna Maggie. Bron motioned further up to a newer grave. "And there are Mum and Dad. They're in together."

Ally raised an eyebrow. "Jackie was okay with your dad being buried with your mum?"

"I suppose," Bron started. She hadn't really thought about it. "Dad had already paid for a double grave when Mum died, and when it came time to bury him, it wasn't like any of us had any spare cash lying around. Besides, my mum is next to Dad's mum, so I guess he figured they would all be together."

Ally seemed to be sorting it out in her own mind. "I remember Nanna Maggie," she said softly. "She didn't like me."

Bron chuckled, raising a hand to her bare shoulder to shield the bite of the hot sun. "She didn't like most people, so don't lose sleep—"

The unexpected roar of a motorbike flying across the main road interrupted her. It was speeding, no more than twenty kilometres too fast, but fast enough to be perilous. Her mind spun just as it did when she had seen or heard anything similar in the last three months. That was the thing about triggers. They were easy to pull once the gun had been shot the first time. Libby had died and suddenly Bron was noticing car accidents everywhere—late night reruns of medical procedurals, the news and Facebook.

"Do you think your dad thought he wouldn't remarry when he bought the double grave?" Ally wondered, drawing Bron back to the conversation at hand.

"I don't know."

"And what about Jackie? Where will she be buried?"

The thought of burying her second mother made Bron dizzy. "I don't really want to think about that right now," she rasped.

"Of course," Ally said, realizing she'd put her foot in it. "I'm sorry I asked."

They fell into a comfortable silence until Ally said, "Next time we should bring flowers to your parents too. And Nanna Maggie."

Jackie already does, Bron thought, but Ally's intention was sweet, so instead Bron whispered, "yes."

There was something about standing there at Libby's grave with Ally that was more upsetting than Bron could've imagined. Was it because her sister had loved Ally so dearly, just as much as she had loved Bron?

They needed to leave. Bron's shoulders were burning, her mouth was parched, and her feet were a putrid russet colour from the mess of dry soil that had caked onto her thongs when she'd stepped out of the car. But it wasn't any of those three things that made her vision glassy. It was the intense, horrible wave of acknowledgment that washed over her. There was her entire family, the one she'd been born into, all of them gone. There, beneath her feet, but...gone. She'd known this for months. It had been one of the dreadful thoughts that had travelled with her on that Virgin Australia flight from Boston to Sydney hours after she'd learned about the accident. Somewhere over the North Pacific Ocean, she'd reached for a sickness bag, blaming it on the heady cocktail of turbulence and profound grief. But again, that needy, ugly sensation of homesickness twisted in her stomach.

"Can we go?" she asked, the question scraping against her throat.

Ally tried to meet her eyes, but she'd already dropped her Aviators back down on the bridge of her nose.

"Yeah," Ally said. "Of course."

Bron shut the driver's door behind her, grateful she'd left the window open. The second she slumped into the seat, a violent sting caught her arm. "Fuck!" she cried, twisting to meet the shining, silver buckle of her seat belt. Ally was staring at her, obviously shocked by the outburst. Nausea washed over Bron. It was threatening and overwhelming. She gripped the back of her arm where it had been seared. "Watch your seat belt buckle. It's on fire," she murmured, a tear escaping from the corner of her eye.

Ally clicked her tongue, oblivious. "On fire, eh?" she teased. "Thought we were over the Ally the Arsonist jabs?"

The black strap of Bron's seat belt wasn't giving. She pulled again, more firmly. It was locked. She grunted.

"Just be gentle," Ally chuckled. "Pull it slowly."

Bron let go of the seat belt and sat back. She closed her eyes. A choked sob escaped. Silent tears followed, flowing in desperate release. They were hot on her burning cheeks. She stung, all over.

Ally shifted on her seat, tucking a leg beneath herself, turning toward Bron. They sat like that for a long moment, until Bron's fast-falling tears slowed. She lifted her sunglasses and wiped at her cheeks, chin and jawline. She made a sound of disgust, belittling her outburst.

"Just take little breaths," Ally suggested.

Bron slapped the top of the scorching steering wheel in frustration. An ache shot from the heel of her palm to her wrist. She let it fall heavily into her lap. More tears fell, gentler this time, an underwhelming, less impressive aftermath.

"Are you okay?"

Bron wet her lips. "That was the first time I've been there since the funeral."

"Oh, Bron. You should have said something." Ally's hand reached out, and Bron turned her own hand over in her lap, expecting Ally's hand to find hers. But suddenly Ally's hand, firm and soft, was pressed against Bron's jawline. Her heartbeat quickened and her face flushed. A tear dared to drip from the tip of her nose. Before she could taste it when it fell to her bottom lip, Ally caught it with her thumb.

A cool breeze placated the back of her neck, tattooing goose bumps to her skin. Ally leaned across the console and rested her forehead against Bron's. She released a wanton, troubled breath. Unmoving, Bron felt it wash over her cheek. *What is happening?* Ally's hand pressed more firmly against her jawline, and Bron's breath hitched. When their lips met, Bron gave in.

Ally's mouth was eager but much less dominant, less *entitled*, than Bron would have thought. But she wasn't thinking at all, not when Ally moved closer than she'd ever been. Too close. Ally's other hand slid around to the back of Bron's neck, controlling the gentle kiss. Bron immediately fell into the new rhythm and she heard herself whimper.

Then Ally's tongue swiped across Bron's bottom lip, hungry and unrelenting. Ally's moan, guttural and feral, poured into Bron's mouth. Ally shifted, moving to kneel on her seat. Suddenly realizing Ally's intentions, Bron quickly pulled back, her eyes wide and bloodshot. Ally's eyelids were pressed shut, as if ending the kiss abruptly had pained her.

"I'm sorry," Bron rasped, her entire body trembling. She dropped her gaze, only for it to land on Ally's full, heaving chest.

"I'm not," Ally whispered, opening her eyes. "I've wanted to do that since I was like…fifteen."

I know you have. "I can't," she said simply.

Ally's hand on her jawline had receded, but the one at the back of her neck remained. Her fingers splayed against her scalp. "I'm not looking for anything serious," Ally husked. Her fingertips trailed up into the bottom of Bron's loose bun. "I think you know that. But we can make this…not serious. If you want," Ally finished.

What Ally proposed was simple—in theory.

When Bron didn't respond, Ally nodded. "Yeah, okay then. It's not like it's the first time you've said no to me."

The memory of seventeen-year-old Ally coming on to her was hazy, but she remembered exactly how the conversation had ended. Bron searched for something to say to fill the uncomfortable silence. "Libby adored you," she tried.

Ally's head snapped around, her entire disposition changing. "What has Libby got to do with what just happened?" Her eyes were a black maelstrom of grief and anger. She was far more complex and intelligent than she allowed others to perceive. The notion was as unnerving as it was fascinating. Ally's reactions were intensifying with the passing of each day, pushing them further into dangerous territory where blame and guilt drew fault lines, fracturing the surface of amity.

Bron pulled at her seat belt, *gently*, and started the car. They had passed the telegraph pole a kilometre back on Gibson Street when Ally spoke up. "We don't have to pretend, you know. You can say something."

"Say something about what?"

"I know that's the pole. Dan and I passed it twice last week."

"Oh."

"He told me they're Jackie's flowers."

Bron swallowed. "Right." Of course he had.

Ally sighed. "I can still remember how old Jackie looked when she came to tell me about Libby." She paused. "I mean, I've lost my dad, but Libby was an entirely different kind of loss.

You expect old people to die, but someone like Libby…It's like all of the joy just goes out of the world. And the worst part, the *worst part*, was not being able to say good-bye. I know none of us did. The impact killed her and she was gone instantly. But I was so close, Bron. Three months. What kind of shitty joke is that? You spend your whole life loving someone and then shit happens like it did and life just fucks you over in the worst way possible."

You spend your whole life loving someone.

Bron's grip tightened on the steering wheel, complete and total cognizance dawning upon her. Had Ally *loved* Libby?

CHAPTER SIX

Bron was surprised to hear soft rapping against her opened bedroom door. She thought everybody had gone to bed an hour ago.

"Hey." Ally smiled from the doorway. "I'm sorry about earlier today."

Bron turned in her desk chair. She gently placed her pencil down against the drawing paper. "Really, Ally," she whispered. "It's fine."

But it wasn't fine. She'd pushed the memory of Ally reaching for her over the console of her old Toyota to the far recesses of her mind.

Ally leaned against the doorjamb and picked at the peeling paint. "I was just wondering if you're planning on being here, you know, working from home, the day after tomorrow?"

Bron drew her gaze away from the obviousness of Ally's dark nipples in just a ribbed, white singlet and stared down at the partially completed draft she'd been working on all day.

"I think so," she murmured. "Why?"

"Well, Jackie's going out to Blackheath to watch Annie's swimming carnival all day on Tuesday, and I heard you say that you're thinking of going over to join her in the afternoon. I just needed someone to…" She hesitated. "My parole officer is coming by around eleven on Tuesday morning. I have to take the day off work to be here, and I'd…I don't know. I'd kind of like it if someone else would be here."

Bron shifted and threw an arm around the back of her desk chair. "That's soon. You've only been here a week."

"It's a fortnightly thing from this point on."

"And out of the blue visits to catch you out?"

"Yeah." Ally smiled. "Those too."

Bron nodded. "Right. Well, I have a Skype meeting in the early hours of Tuesday morning, so I'll be around, working…" She smiled politely and turned back to her desk.

In her peripheral vision, Bron watched Ally shift from foot to foot, and then step into the room. Her old bed springs squeaked with Ally's weight. She raised her gaze. The pitch-black sky reminded her of the late hour, prompting her to wonder why Ally hadn't gone to sleep when everyone else had.

The quiet wasn't as strange as it had been a week ago—before Ally had confronted her, before the cemetery saga. Just above the tops of the gumtrees, the Northern Star shone brilliantly. In Boston she never saw the night sky so clean and clear. She would have to drive up to Salem, or even further to Ipswich, if she wanted to see a crisp sky blanketed with stars. But she rarely left the city.

Ally broke the silence. "You're a hard worker, Bron."

Bent over her drawing board, she shrugged.

"You're always up here, drawing away. What is it that you're working on?"

"Just another children's picture book."

"What's it about?"

She turned to Ally and tapped her pencil against the back of the chair. "It's about a little girl who solves mysteries at school."

"What does she look like?"

Bron reached across her desk and picked up the sketchbook filled with drawings just for her own reference. Ally flipped through it for a few moments. "They're really great. I remember you drawing like this."

Bron raised an eyebrow. "You remember?"

"Yeah. When Annie was born, Lib had one of your books. I used to read it to Annie all of the time."

Ally handed her the sketchbook, and Bron placed it back on the pile of drawing pads. "You work hard too, Al."

Ally shifted where she sat on the edge of the bed. "I've been thinking of building a cubby house for Annie."

"Oh?"

"Nothing fancy. I'm not *great* with construction, but I can put something rough together."

"I'm sure she'd love it."

"I haven't told her yet," Ally added. "But we're going to the hardware on the weekend. I'll let her pick a paint colour and stuff."

She could picture Annie, armed with so many choices in the hardware store. It wasn't going to be a cheap cubby house if Ally let Annie have her way—and Bron knew that Ally would. She clicked her tongue. "The materials will be expensive. Let me help you out with the cost."

Ally shook her head, adamant. "It's just a cubby house. Besides, I owe you enough as it is."

An uncomfortable silence fell upon them, turning the air in the room stale. She decided it was best not to push it with the money issue, but she couldn't help but worry that Ally was being too generous with funds she didn't actually have to begin with. The cemetery flowers and now a cubby house. Bron couldn't deny that, however reckless Ally was with what little money she had, her intentions came from a good place. Her eyes fell to the Annie tattoo that decorated Ally's chest. Maybe she'd been wrong to assume the tattoo was a guilt card to be played whenever Ally drew a bad hand.

Ally pushed off the bed and stopped at the door. "I'm sorry I put you through all of that today."

"Ally—"

"If I'd known, I wouldn't have asked you to take me. I know you're still a mess." She paused, and that dreadful, wild ache seized Bron's heart. "We're all a mess right now, but we'll get it together soon. I'm sure of it."

She'd heard the same assurance many times before—from Jackie, from Annie's psychologist, from strangers who had known Libby. But there was something real and believable about the way Ally said it. Maybe it was because, at the end of the day, they were both such a mess because they shared one thing in common—for the longest time they'd both been separated from their closest friend. Oceans, prison bars, it didn't really matter. Borders were borders, and borders had kept both of them from Libby in her final years and her last days. Their heartache came from the same dark place. So if Ally could at least pretend to be one step closer to moving on, there was no reason Bron couldn't do the same.

* * *

At nine o'clock on Tuesday morning, Bron stumbled down the hallway on autopilot. The bedroom doors were all open but nobody was upstairs. Why was it so humid *so early*? Why had Jackie and Annie left without waking her? Why had she stayed up and continued working another *two hours* after that Skype meeting with her editor at Yellowstone? In the future she wasn't going to accommodate three a.m. videoconferences. Besides, could the company actually call it a conference when her editor hadn't even had the courtesy to Skype Bron from the office? She was still irritated by it. If Yellowstone considered an editor criticizing an illustrator's drafts over video chat while in line at Starbucks a *conference*, she would really have to consider their definition of the 'formal' dress code at next year's company Christmas party. No more middle-of-the-night meetings. She needed to stop putting other people first. It had been her only New Year's resolution, but any trace of *that* had certainly gone out the window back in August after the accident. A lighter workload with Yellowstone was a heavenly thought, and she'd be able to afford it too with the pay packet MIT was offering for only four two-hour lectures a week and a couple of seminars.

Morning lectures meant she'd be free to pick Annie up from school each day, spend weekends with her on the Common or in one of Boston's many museums. Perhaps she'd even dump Yellowstone for a while once she settled in at MIT. Let Yellowstone see what they're taking for granted, she thought.

In a daze, she went into the bathroom and closed the door behind her. "Jesus!" she shrieked, her cheeks flaming instantly.

Ally stood before the mirror, completely naked but for the black cotton hugging her hips and the surprised expression she wore. Her short hair was wet, slicked back, her breasts bare and nipples dark, just as Bron had guessed. But it was the burn scar, the mottled and taut patch of skin that drew Bron's attention to Ally's navel. All Bron knew was that Ally had been burned during her time as a volunteer firefighter. The scar was so much larger than she'd thought it would be, a faded pink against Ally's perfect skin.

Sensing Ally's stare, Bron immediately checked herself out of her stupor. "I...You didn't lock the door..."

Ally pressed a hip against the sink. An eyebrow arched. "So? You didn't knock."

Bron quickly exited, her ears ringing. She closed her bedroom door and sat down on her bed, rubbing at her face in a vigorous attempt to wake herself. Embarrassment flushed through her in a second wave. Her neck was hot and her hands were clammy. She heard the bathroom door open and then the click of Libby's bedroom door. She sat, unmoving. Quiet.

Everybody was gone. It was just the two of them. The house was so empty, devoid of Annie's squeals and Jackie's whistling, that Bron could actually hear it creak. During the day. While there was *sunlight*. It was a rare phenomenon.

She walked briskly back toward the bathroom, desperately hoping for Ally to stay in her room until Bron had hidden herself away. She turned the bathroom lock, the heavy snap of sliding metal brasher than usual. Undoubtedly, Ally would have heard it and assumed Bron was making a point.

When she flicked off the hair dryer twenty minutes later, her freshly-washed hair dry enough that it wouldn't dampen the back of her T-shirt, she could hear a muffled, male voice responding to Ally's always-amplified questions. She made her way down to the kitchen. When she stopped in the doorway, Ally's gaze lifted from the burly man sitting in Jackie's spot at the kitchen table.

"Bron, this here is my parole officer, Barry."

She moved across the room to shake Barry's hand and introduced herself.

Barry smiled warmly. "I read your letter of support for Ally's parole, and the one your mother wrote too. Really helped us out in the beginning there."

She could feel her face warming again. She noticed Ally avert her gaze at the mention of the letter. Barry motioned toward Ally. "Bet you're regretting it now that you're stuck with her." In true form, Ally had shrunken down into her chair, completely relaxed and confident. The insecure girl who had stood in her bedroom doorway two nights before was nowhere to be seen.

"No regrets. She loves it," Ally jumped in. "Want a cuppa, Baz?"

Bron busied herself putting the kettle on. She waved good morning to Tammy, who sat outside the screen door, tail wagging, desperate for their new visitor's attention.

Barry and Ally made small talk while Bron listened intently. This wasn't their first meeting. Apparently he'd been the one to get the ball rolling on Ally's parole, but after she'd submitted the application, she'd been assigned a different parole officer while he was on long service leave.

"Has she been a handful to manage?" he asked.

Bron smiled. *Manage.* He'd found the perfect job description for this role Jackie and Bron had volunteered to take on, a role which demanded they made sure Ally met curfew and didn't attempt to burn anything with greater consequence than a steak. "No," she chuckled. "No more of a handful than usual."

Ally scoffed and stood, moving to get the milk from the fridge. As the kettle whistled, Tammy barked loudly, her black snout concaving the fly screen of the laundry door. Bron shushed her, knowing there was no point.

Barry laughed, pulling open the screen door. Bron watched from the corner of the kitchen as he calmed Tammy with a scratch behind her ears.

She smiled, watching Tammy lap up the attention before she returned to making the tea.

The potent feeling of being watched immediately drew her attention from the kettle. Ally leaned against the opposite counter, staring at Bron, her eyes intense and searching.

Bron's skin prickled. "What's wrong?"

Ally's voice was low. "Nothing." She continued to stare. "You're just very attractive."

Thrown by the compliment, Bron looked away.

"How much water you been getting in the tank?" Barry called out.

It wasn't that Ally was moving closer that unnerved her. It was the way that, as she placed the milk down in front of Bron, Ally looked out to see if Barry could see them from where he was standing—as though she knew something Bron did not.

"Oh, the tank's old. We're on town water these days," Bron explained, trying desperately to ignore Ally's nearness, but she could feel the heat radiating from her body.

And she smelled *wonderful.*

Barry was still talking. Bron just caught the tail end as he said, "... My old man's got a water tank down in South Australia. Bloody pain in the ass, those things."

In pursuit of three mugs, Bron's fingers wrapped around the handle of the top cupboard. Ally covered Bron's hand and pulled open the cupboard. Bron shifted closer to the counter, away from Ally, struggling not to let Ally press closer.

As Ally grabbed the mugs, Bron dropped a teabag into each, barely listening as Barry muttered on about the mudbrick home his father had built. Ally's breath warmed the shell of Bron's ear when she called out a reply to their visitor.

Bron's hands trembled as she lifted the kettle and unskilfully poured boiling water into the mugs. She swore under her breath as the paper tab of a teabag slipped over the lip of one of the mugs and into the weak, steaming tea. As Bron reached across the sink for a teaspoon to scoop up the floating label, Ally pressed closer.

"Don't," Bron murmured, her shoulders shifting.

The instant Ally's warm hand came to rest just above Bron's hip, so gentle and timid, she jumped and faced her. It had been so long since her body had been so responsive to another woman's touch.

"Ally," she whispered. "*Don't.*"

Ally looked down at her with a muddled expression. "What?" she husked. The hurt in her voice was palpable.

Why is she staring at me like I've led her on? Bron thought she'd been clear.

"Come on," Ally said, her eyes on Bron's lips. "I know how you looked at me upstairs."

She blushed hotly, remembering Ally's naked body. "It was an accident," she whispered, peering at the back door.

Ally licked her lips. "I know, but you still—"

As the back door opened, Ally shifted, putting a great deal of space between herself and Bron. "Black or white, Baz?"

"Just a splash of milk, thanks."

Ally placed Barry's tea and an unopened carton of milk on the table in front of him. "There you go." She plonked down into her chair and spread her legs widely beneath the table.

Bron reached for the milk. "Here, I can open that," she politely insisted.

Ally reached across the table and swatted her hands away.

"He may be male, but he's not an invalid," Ally playfully reprimanded her. "He can open a milk carton."

As she sat down, Bron stole a glance at Barry, shaking his head with a grin as he popped open the milk carton.

Bron wondered if Ally realised just how lucky she was that her parole officer had the stomach to digest her sense of humour. It made Bron uneasy watching how far Ally pushed it with him. It made her uneasy watching how far Ally pushed it with *everything*.

He pulled out a file and scribbled down a few notes about Ally's week working with Daniel. As she explained her temporary role in the business, beneath the table her foot tapped against Bron's, once, twice, and a third time. Bron glanced up, but Ally was focused on Barry's approving nods as he jotted down key words for his report. She waited for Ally to tease her again, but it never came.

"And your plans for the future?" he prompted.

Ally smiled. "Let's just get past Christmas, eh, Boss?"

He grinned, shaking his pen at her. "Not good enough. I'll give you until the New Year to find something more permanent and goal-oriented, but as long as Mr. Lee obtains his painting licence, I think working with the family is a good way to get you back out there."

When he was finished, the women walked him out to his car. Bron stood back on the veranda to wave while Ally followed him down the steps.

"Has she been keeping curfew?" he called back to Bron.

Ally looked up to the veranda. She shoved her hands into her pockets, and for the first time that morning, her eyes cast over with a glimmer of panic as she stared at Bron, waiting.

Bron paused, allowing Ally to flounder in anxiety for a moment longer. It was a rare thing to feel in control of Ally. She liked it. "Well, I caught her up until two the other morning watching reruns of *Law and Order*. Does that count as breaking curfew?"

Ally visibly relaxed and she felt…powerful.

Barry waved his hand in dismissal. "As long as she's not getting any ideas from it, I won't send her back to Oberon any time soon."

Bron went back inside, and it wasn't long before Barry was gone and Ally's work boots were thudding up the back steps. The fly screen swung halfway open, and Ally remained in the doorway, her demeanour unusually pensive. "I'm walking into town," she said shortly.

At the kitchen table, Bron stopped typing one-handed. She placed the slice of toast pinched between the fingers of the other hand on her plate, and closed the lid of her laptop. "Al, I didn't mean to push you away, but he was just outside…"

Ally groaned dramatically. "For fuck's sake, Bron! I just gave you a compliment, okay? You're beautiful, that's all. *That's it.* Jesus Christ, we don't have to have a fucking discussion about *everything.*"

Offended, Bron sat back in her chair, and folded her arms. "Why are you suddenly so dirty with me? You put me in an uncomfortable position!"

Ally offered a frustrated gasp.

Bron pressed further. "I don't know what I've done wrong, Ally. I didn't mean to walk in on you this morning, and what happened at the cemetery the other day was..." She faltered. "We both know it was just one of those things."

Ally's expression tightened. She pointed at Bron, waving her finger. "You frustrate the hell out of me," she said decisively.

Bron tilted her head, her eyes widening. "*I* frustrate *you*? Why would you even do something like that when your parole officer is here?" she exclaimed. "To make me feel uncomfortable? To intimidate me?"

Ally looked down, brows furrowed. She scoffed, as though Bron had missed something colossal.

"*What*, Ally?" Bron demanded, exasperated. "What is it that I *do* that could possibly frustrate you so much?"

Ally shook her head. "Forget it."

Bron shrugged. "Fine."

The back screen slammed behind Ally. "Fine!" she shouted back.

Bron couldn't concentrate after the argument. Every few moments she caught herself looking up from her work desk, peering out the window to the driveway, wondering where Ally had gone. *Once this page is finished, you can drive over to the pools at Blackheath*, she compromised with herself. She needed a break.

As she detailed the cityscape on page seventeen with office windows and rooftop spires, she thought about Ally, about the obvious attraction between them. There wasn't any point in denying it. It was there and it wasn't going away. But Ally was like Jekyll and Hyde. She could go from virtuous to irritable in the blink of an eye. Her moods were dizzying.

There was a common denominator that seemed to set Ally off each time—rejection. She certainly didn't take rejection lightly. So why, if Bron had already rejected her once, had Ally made another advance that morning in the kitchen? Was it simply because they were both gay and Bron was…convenient? *Did she think I was playing hard to get? Am I sending a vibe?* She needed to make it clear to Ally that *it* wasn't going to happen, however good she guessed *it* would be.

Before she was even close to finishing page seventeen, Annie was back with Jackie just after lunchtime proudly wearing three orange Good Try ribbons pinned to her Lycra swimsuit.

"I beat two boys from *Year Three* in backstroke!" Annie bragged as she removed her ribbons with great reverence. She held them to the fridge with the special glass magnets Bron had sent from her brief time in Chicago years before.

"That's just wonderful," Bron exclaimed, pressing her lips tightly to Annie's hairline as the little girl stood before the fridge, admiring her ribbons. The overpowering scents of chlorine and sunscreen still lingered in her hair and on her skin.

Bron cut her sandwich and offered Annie the larger half. "You're back very early!" she commented.

Jackie looked at her with apology. "The rest of the afternoon were relays for the bigger kids. They said parents could sign the littles out, and she was just dying to show you her ribbons."

"That's okay," Bron said. "I was about to drive over anyway."

"Sorry we didn't wake you before we left this morning," Jackie added. "I went to the loo around four and saw your light still on. Wanted to let you have a little bit of a sleep in." Jackie nodded down at Annie. "I know it's hard with…work."

"I'm coping," Bron lied, wondering if she'd ever learn how to balance the demands of a career and a child—alone. Libby had been a full-time high school teacher and she'd managed. Thousands of single parents did on a daily basis. But Bron had been thrown into the deep end without ever learning the basics.

All she could do was hope that dog paddling would keep her head above water, even if she made it to the finish line in last place. She had no other choice. It was the hand she'd been dealt, and she was going to accept it. Do not pass go. Do not collect two hundred dollars.

But being granted sole custody of Annie hadn't been anything like drawing the jail card in a board game. Annie was better than rolling a double six or pulling a Draw Four from the top of the Uno deck. As her niece described the terrifying tilt of the diving block she'd jumped from earlier that day, she scarfed down her entire lunch for the first time since the accident. Bron was delighted.

"Can you come watch me while I practice in the pool?" Annie pleaded.

She agreed, wondering how long it was going to take Annie to realize she couldn't swim a great distance in their two by three kiddie pool. "Go and fill it up, but don't get in until I come out, okay?"

When Annie was out of earshot, Bron said, "She just ate half of a BLT in under three minutes."

"It's Ally," Jackie said in astonishment. "She's made my little girl healthy again."

She allowed Jackie's words to sink in. While she'd kept Annie alive and functioning after the accident, the promise of Ally's return, and then her divine intervention, had been the thing that had put colour back into Annie cheeks. She had to admit Ally was good for Annie.

"I'm knackered," Jackie sighed. "We were in such a rush this morning I forgot my umbrella. If I'd have forgotten my sunhat too, I'm sure I'd have passed out from heatstroke."

"I'm sorry," she said. "I should have taken her. I know you don't mix well with the heat."

"Nonsense." Jackie waved her hand as much to cool herself down as to brush aside Bron's apology. "You've got so much work on your plate, now that you've decided to stay until way after Christmas."

She rolled her eyes. She'd made no such promise. "How do you do that?"

Jackie grinned. "Do what, darling?"

"Try to guilt trip me into staying even longer while I'm in the middle of an apology."

"Would I do a thing like that?" Jackie said with a grin, but her eyes were hazy. She'd always been so easy to read, unlike their father. It would hurt Jackie deeply if she took Annie back to Boston for good, and Bron *hated* that.

"Go watch your niece. I'm off for a Nanna nap."

Bron stood from the table and got some water. Outside she could see Annie standing patiently next to the kiddie pool, chucking her innovative pool toys into the water. In went the gardening can, an old Coke bottle, Safari Barbie and a tennis ball. The garden hose snaked wildly across the mat of the knee-deep pool since Annie always turned the hose pressure up far too high.

"Annie," she called out the window. "You can get in, I'm watching."

She looked down into her glass. The filter tap was releasing water at a rate of approximately four drops per minute. She thought of the water pressure in Boston, her perfect shower and the abundance of water. With one eye on Annie, she reached into the freezer for ice, filling her glass to the brim with the frozen blocks before she headed outside.

Annie wrestled with the twisting, possessed garden hose while Tammy barked fanatically at the performance. Bron climbed down the steps of the back veranda and turned off the tap. Annie fist pumped as the hose gradually fell limp. "I claim victory," she yelled at the lifeless hose and plonked back down, the water level rising to just below her shoulders.

Bron set her glass in the small spot of shade on the edge of the veranda while Annie attempted to float, the sunscreen Jackie lathered her in earlier that day forming a halo of oil around her little body.

"Where's Ally?" Annie asked.

"Ally went for a walk a few hours ago."

Annie sat up. "When will she be back?"

As Bron sat down on the edge of the veranda, the blunt head of a nail in one of the veranda panels scorched the back of her thigh. She shifted in the sun. "I don't know, Annie."

"I wanna show her my ribbons."

"And I'm sure she'll love them when she sees them."

Annie contemplated this for a moment. "Did you ever win any medals?"

"Yes. I've won a few for my drawings."

Annie stared at her, completely unimpressed. "No, I mean for real stuff, like swimming or running."

"Oh…" Bron chuckled. "Then no, not for *real stuff*. Not that I can recall." She thought for a moment. "Your mum did, though."

At the mention of her mother, Annie immediately pinched her nose and pitched forward into the water, submerging herself in the twenty-five inches of water. Bron sighed. She shouldn't have expected any different, but she couldn't help but wonder how long it would take until she could mention Libby without Annie running from the room.

A moment passed. Annie did not pop back up. Sudden panic flared in Bron. She leaped forward, the rough, splintery edge of the veranda scraping against the backs of her bare thighs. The glass of ice tipped off the edge of the veranda, and she heard it smash upon the dirt floor below. In a second, she fell to her knees, reached into the pool, and hoisted Annie up by her armpits with such crazed strength that the child stood in the water on both feet. Annie's wide, shocked eyes bore down into Bron's frightened ones.

"Why did you do that?" Bron demanded, the edge of her voice tearing.

Tammy moved closer, quietly observing Annie and Bron stare at each other, both breathless.

Annie's frightened eyes watered. "I…" She drew back a sob. "I was just trying to beat my record."

Bron swallowed, her heartbeat slowing. "No more of that, okay?" she rasped. "No more, Annie."

Annie released a deep breath. In her tight hold, Bron could feel her frame quivering. She diverted her gaze from Bron's intense stare and looked down at Tammy. Two lone tears fell, but her face was blank, like she had no idea that she was crying. As though sensing the intensity of the moment, Tammy sat down next to Bron, her gaze darting curiously between the two. For the first time since she'd come home, Bron wasn't sure how to read Annie. She smoothed a hand over Annie's wet hair, ran her thumbs over her cheeks. She was so beautiful, so delicate. But she was haunted too.

"Are you okay?" Bron whispered. She tilted her head lower to catch her eye. "I'm sorry I upset you by mentioning Mummy."

Annie closed her eyes tightly. Bron waited patiently, loosening her grip on Annie's tiny hips. When Annie opened her eyes, she looked…better. "That's okay," she said softly.

She relaxed. "Are you sure, sweetheart?"

"Yes."

Bron shook her gently, as she always did when she was trying to get a giggle out of the six-year-old. The corners of Annie's mouth twitched. "Annie, someday thinking about Mummy will be better than okay."

Annie simply nodded and shifted from Bron's hold. "I'm going to play Olympic games now," she said and picked up Safari Barbie.

Bron stood for a moment, looking down at Annie, her mind vacant. The little girl was deep in conversation with Tammy, informing their retriever of the rules of the fifty-meter freestyle. Annie had moved on, but Bron had not. Her head was swimming. She would tell Annie's psychologist about the incident. She would describe it, but how could she ever manage to convey the utter terror of the moment?

"Hey, Ally!"

Bron's gaze shot up. Annie was out of the pool in an instant, her disposition completely revived. She reached for her towel. "Boy, have I got something to show you!" she exclaimed, already halfway to the house. "I've got ribbons!"

Ally leaned against the railing of the veranda, laughing as Annie raced inside. She stopped when her gaze fell to the dirt floor below. "Is that glass?" she said, her eyes focused on the small, glimmering puddle at the base of the veranda.

"Oh, shit," Bron cursed. "I bumped it and got distracted," she said, refraining from elaborating any further.

They both reached down, picking out the largest pieces first.

"Careful," Ally mumbled, motioning with a flick of her wrist for Bron to move away. "Let me. Go get a dustpan before Tammy decides to come traipsing over here."

"Not all of it's glass. Some of it's ice," Bron said.

"I can see that." Ally picked out a dust-coated, melting ice block and skimmed it across the lawn.

As she moved toward the house under Ally's instruction, Bron looked back. For the life of her, she couldn't remember the last time she'd broken a glass and somebody else had offered to clean up the mess.

CHAPTER SEVEN

Annie's psychologist, Diana Thompsett, had a brilliant office. The walls were a messy wonderland of children's artwork and empowering posters with funky fonts. But the office was also brilliant in the sense that it inspired Bron in a way that Annie's decorated classroom hadn't managed to at the parent/teacher interviews the month before. As a children's illustrator, Bron knew just how profoundly images and carefully selected colours could impact children—especially troubled children. Diana's office was free of rules and completely unpretentious, just a warm and welcoming safe space.

This was their first session—alone—to discuss Annie's progress, and Bron was anxious. Although Diana had to be at least fifteen years younger than Bron and a novice in the profession, she made up for her inexperience with a kind of confidence that, in her forty years, Bron had only ever seen in a few people. When they had first met, Bron had been surprised to find that, for a child psychologist, Diana's manner was unequivocally abrupt. Bron doubted Annie would open up to the fiery redhead, but she'd been pleasantly surprised after watching the two of them interact before a session started or when Annie returned to the waiting room after the hour concluded. Annie seemed more comfortable and relaxed with Diana than Bron was herself.

Left alone in Diana's office while she finished up outside with a previous consult, Bron's gaze wandered across the bookshelf. Although the bottom two rows were shielded by an oversized green beanbag, the majority of the picture books on the higher shelves were related to anxiety and bullying. There were a few other subjects that stood out in the titles. Family. Loss. At least five book spines had some variation of grandma and gone in the title. She couldn't fight the narcissistic urge to scan the titles for one of her own picture books. Evidently her most celebrated mass-market picture book series about a privileged little Manhattan rich girl wasn't perceived by Diana to have much of an impact on a grieving child's life. It was ironic. Even if Bron's picture books couldn't comfort another anguished child, the royalties she earned from that particular series paid for Annie's sessions with Diana. The cycle of life, Bron mused.

The door clicked open and Diana smiled warmly down at Bron, her expression etched in surprised.

"Is something wrong?" Bron asked.

"No, no," Diana assured her, closing the door behind her and taking a seat across from Bron. "Annie mentioned you're heading home to the US in the near future, so I wasn't expecting you. I didn't know you would be the one attending the consult."

So we're getting right to it. She forced a smile. "I'm not quite sure she understands the concept of another country, but—"

"I think she understands the concept." Diana tilted her head, appraising Bron. She looked down at the notes in front of her, peeling back pages, which Bron assumed to be about Annie. "I don't want to jeopardise the progress Annie has made with me— these past few weeks, especially—so I'd like to keep whatever is discussed between us today confidential. This is very important so that Annie and I can continue to make strides each week."

Strides. Suddenly realising Diana was waiting for her response, Bron quickly replied, "Oh, of course."

Diana sat back in her chair. "Annie's quite distraught that you're leaving."

Bron raised an eyebrow and smiled in disbelief. "Distraught?"

"Is that surprising?"

"Yeah, it is. To be honest, we haven't really brought it up much in front of her. When I do go back to Boston, it'll only be for a short time, a month or so. I was on a flight out as soon as I heard about the accident and there are things I need to take care of with work."

Diana looked relieved. "So you've decided to move back to Australia?"

"Oh, I'm coming back here. But I'm not sure how long I'll be staying upon my return." Bron hesitated. "I've actually been offered a teaching position at the Massachusetts Institute of Technology, and it's too good to decline. So, I have two options. I stay here permanently, or I move Annie to Boston with me."

"You're considering uprooting her life here to take her to the US?"

Bron nodded, gathering from Diana's sour expression that she clearly did not approve of Option Number Two.

Diana clicked her tongue. "I'd like to ask about Ally."

Bron reminded herself to keep all traces of judgment from her voice. "Ally was my sister's best friend. She's just been released on parole and she's staying with us."

Diana smiled. "Annie adores her."

She nodded, her gaze dropping to the fluffy rainbow rug by Diana's desk. "They're very close."

Diana drew a deep breath. "I'm simply concerned that if you return to the States, even for a short while, and Ally's presence fails to remain consistent, Annie will withdraw. It seems that you and Ally are huge influences on her development—her happiness too."

She swallowed the lump in her throat. *Way to pile on the guilt, Di.*

"You have sole custody of Annie?" Diana asked.

"Yes."

"So what happens when you return to the States?"

Diana's condescending head tilt was beginning to irritate her. Bron hesitated for a moment before she spoke. "I think it's best for Annie to stay here with her grandmother and my brother. And Ally." She continued over the dryness in her mouth. "Like I said, I need to assess my options. I'll take stock of the schools for Annie and decide if my apartment is big enough for the both of us."

Diana hummed her acknowledgment and the room fell quiet while she skimmed her notes. "So, I opened a dialogue with Annie about the accident. For the most part she seems to be developing a healthy response to the trauma, the memories…"

Bron crossed her legs, her trembling hand sliding between her thighs. "Has she spoken about Libby?"

Diana nodded. "I broached the subject last month."

"I'm sorry, you said last month?"

"You seem surprised."

"I am." She paused, choosing her words carefully. "There was an incident the other day."

"Mmm?"

"Annie was swimming—"

"She told me about the carnival."

"After the carnival. We have a kiddie pool for her to muck around in. I was watching her, standing right there by the pool. I mentioned Libby and she just—"

"Clammed up?"

Bron swallowed. "No. She ducked under the water and held herself there for too long. I panicked and reefed her out. She said she was trying to beat her own record, but I wasn't having any of that."

Diana sat forward. "How long was she under?"

Bron pinched the bridge of her nose. "Long enough."

"Long enough for what?"

Why were psychologists always so afraid of putting words in people's mouths? She resisted the strong urge to roll her eyes.

"Long enough to drown out any thoughts of her mother. Long enough for it to register as more than just a way to get me to shut up about Libby."

Diana was quiet for a long moment. "Annie has never struck me as high-dependency."

Bron sighed. "Me neither. But I can't stop thinking about it. And now every little thing she does…I'm watching like a hawk."

Diana clasped her hands together and leaned her elbows on her knees. "Look, Bron, the thing with the pool…These kinds of things aren't always what they seem. Any kid who has experienced what Annie has is going to have moments which seem to us, as adults, more dangerous than they actually are. You're implying she intended to hurt herself, but Annie knew you were right there, watching her, that you would reach for her. I know you can't look at this the way an outsider can, but what this incident tells me is that Annie trusts you very much. If anything of the sort happens again, then we'll look at it more closely. But what I think happened is that you inadvertently triggered her with the topic of her deepest loss, her most profound trauma, on a day that had been kind to her. My opinion is that Annie was rejecting the dialogue you were proposing rather than attempting to harm herself. She'd won ribbons in a race, she'd been commended for doing good, and she'd exhausted herself swimming all day long. The last thing she probably wanted was to talk about Libby. She just wanted to have a day for herself."

Bron looked out the second-story window. "And I took that from her."

"No," Diana stated firmly. "She's already moved on from what happened that day. It's forgotten. *I'm* not worried, so you should stop fretting. But I'm going to be blunt with you, Bron. What I *am* worried about is what happens next year. It's going to be a huge detriment to Annie if you move her to the US, even if it's in a year. You need to think about this very carefully."

"I'm still thinking about how I can make this work."

After a moment, Diana nodded. "Okay."

The rest of what she said fell on deaf ears. While Diana's reassurance about the kiddie pool episode brought Bron a great deal of relief, Diana had very clear opinions about the future prospect of Annie leaving Australia. Would she ever call Boston home again?

As though on autopilot, she made her way down the tree-lined street after the meeting, her mind a conflicting mess. She pulled open the driver's door and sought refuge in the front seat, immediately rolling down the window. A cool afternoon breeze swept over her sweaty neck—a small consolation. *What am I going to do?*

She cradled her head in her hands. She tried to imagine a future where she stayed, and then tried to imagine a future where she went home to Boston—with Annie—against everybody's wishes. The latter was the selfish option, but if she stayed in the mountains, what would that cost her? She had worked so very hard to build a life for herself overseas. Would she be undoing all of that hard work just to make everybody else—her mother, her brother, *Diana*—happy? *And Annie?* Her conscience pressed against her desires. Kids are resilient, Bron thought. Surely Annie would adapt after a while.

It was after five when she stopped at the driveway entrance. Tammy waited patiently on the other side, probably for Daniel, or maybe Jackie had just left for Friday night bingo and taken Annie with her. She looked up the driveway. At the top of the hill, she could see the back tray of Daniel's ute.

And then realisation dawned on her. "Are you waiting for me, Miss Tammy? That's a first!"

Her heart couldn't help but swell a little bit at the unexpected attention. She encouraged Tammy into the passenger seat for the short drive up the hill. She locked the gate behind her, and when she climbed back into the car, she instantly regretted the invitation when she saw blond hair blanketing every inch of the black seat cover.

"Malting season, huh?"

Tammy panted her answer. "Look," she said to Tammy as the car climbed up the hill. Annie and Ally were in the middle of the yard, running in circles. Bron waved when they looked up. "Who's that, Tammy? What are they doing?"

In the middle of the front yard, a revolving sprinkler shot water so high into the sky that the droplets showered down over Ally's head. Annie was inching closer to the sprinkler, the force of the water soaking her more completely as she bent lower. Ally laughed as Annie cupped her tiny hands against the rotating faucets and pulled back a second later, the pressure of the water exploding in her face. Drenched in her school dress, she cackled wildly. Trust Ally to let Annie run around beneath a sprinkler in her school uniform. Thank god she didn't have school tomorrow.

But Bron could deal with laundering a saturated school dress every single weekday if it meant that the kiddie pool lay forgotten around the side of the house for all of eternity. Ally had found a solution without ever knowing there was a problem.

"Aunty Bron, Ally got us a sprinkler!"

She tightened her ponytail, pulling it higher on the top of her head. "I can see that!" She fought the urge to be a buzzkill by pointing out—along with the school uniform issue—just how much water they were wasting. She didn't know if the ability to keep her lips sealed came from a desire to see Annie happy or a desire to impress Ally with her relaxed disposition.

Annie crawled forward across the wet grass. *Oh god, the uniform will be covered in grass stains!* She cupped her hands around the faucet again. Ally reached down and grasped her under the armpits, swinging her tiny body over the top of the fountain a few times. As Annie squealed, Ally looked at Bron, her expression vibrant.

Bron smiled back. Ally was a *good* person. She was never anything but kind to Annie. She loved the little girl. And she was equally as saturated. Her black T-shirt, which was almost a size too big, clung to her abdomen. As she swung Annie over the powerful jet of the sprinkler again, the definition of the muscles in her forearms was prominent. Bron allowed herself a moment to wonder what Ally's body would feel like beneath hers. Hot. Energetic. *Dominant...*

In a daze, she clenched the car keys tighter in her fist. Ally looked over at her again, and their gazes held. Ally's smile faltered. *Caught.*

She started toward the house, feeling Ally's dark stare on her, observant and knowing.

"Want to get wet?" Ally teased as Bron stepped around the perimeter of the saturated grass.

She shook her head and went inside.

"Do you mind if I join you? I come bearing gifts."

Bron craned her head back against the porch swing to find Ally standing contemplatively in the doorway of the house. She lifted her arm, playfully waving one of the glass water bottles Jackie kept refilled with lemon water in the fridge. In her other hand, she had a glass for each of them pinched between two fingers.

Daniel was out with Carly, and Jackie had taken Annie with her to bingo at the bowling club. "I missed last week," her mother had said, truly concerned. "They'll be wondering what's happened to me!" And so Bron and Ally had been left alone to have dinner together. It had surprised Bron how easy it had been to fill an hour talking trivial nonsense with Ally as they ate and cleaned up after themselves. Afterward, Ally had excused herself to shower.

Bron turned so that her back was pressed against the armrest of the swing and folded her legs beneath herself to make room for Ally, who must have mistaken the trepidation in Bron's expression for discomfort. "If you want to be alone while you can, I can just go back inside," she offered, the frosty bottle dangling in her fist.

"Of course not," Bron said, watching as Ally set the bottle down on the small table in front of them.

The porch seat swayed, becoming accustomed to the added weight. As Ally leaned forward to fill their glasses, Bron's eyes tracked how high the hem of Ally's old Beatles T-shirt rode up. She permitted herself three seconds to admire the exposed tops of Ally's naked thighs, the curve where her leg met dark underwear. Bron tried to remember the last time she'd felt confident enough to walk around the house in nothing but her sleep shirt and boy shorts. Probably way back in nineteen-ninety-never.

At the sound of voices, Tammy came around the corner of the wraparound veranda, her chocolate-coloured eyes trained on them.

"Hi, Tammy-girl," Ally sing-songed.

At the encouragement, Tammy sashayed up the steps. Ally beamed at Tammy, and a tingling sensation fired through Bron's body. She bit her lip. Tail wagging, Tammy laid down.

"Jackie said that your appointment with Annie's psych went well."

"Yeah. She's happy with Annie's progress."

"God," Ally drawled, "those cicadas are deafening tonight."

Bron looked out into the darkness. "I hadn't realised until you just said it."

"I suppose it'll *bug* the hell out of you now."

Bron rolled her eyes. "Good one."

Ally sat back and closed her eyes. After a long moment passed, she whispered, "I don't know if it'll ever get old."

"What's that?"

"Just being out. Being happy."

"What did you miss the most? Steak? Alcohol?"

Ally shrugged. "I'm still not sure. Normalcy, I suppose."

"It must have been nice to have Libby visit so often."

Ally nodded, picking at the peeling ink on her shirt.

Silence fell upon them. Bron asked, "Were you in love with my sister?"

Ally's gaze shot up. "No." She exhaled harshly and added, "But I was in love with you."

Thrown by Ally's confession, Bron reached for her glass of lemon water. "Really?" she asked lightly. "In love?"

"Yeah…" Ally said hoarsely. "Fifteen and madly in love with a twenty-two-year-old who wouldn't even give me the time of day." She waved a hand. "I know you all knew."

Bron chuckled, finally meeting her gaze. "I guess it seems so silly now."

Ally's glare was tumultuous. "Does it?"

"Well," she said slowly, trying to alleviate the tension between them, "we all had those older-woman crushes. I fell for my high school art teacher."

Ally was quiet for so long that Bron thought she'd offended her. Eventually Ally spoke up. "Mrs Wrangler? She was thirty years older than you and married with like eight kids."

Bron smiled. "I couldn't help it."

Ally scoffed. "If you're going to set your sights on straight women, at least set an age difference of no more than ten years. The odds are better."

"Sounds like you're talking from experience."

Ally shrugged.

Bron took another sip of water. "It was probably for the best. I'm not ready to settle down with a seventy-year-old wife." Ally didn't say anything to that. She checked her phone. 9:22. She'd have to leave soon to pick up Jackie and Annie. "I heard you had a surprise visitor when I was out last night."

Ally hummed in confirmation that her parole officer had come by. "They're trying to catch me out. But they won't win. I'm doing everything by the book."

Bron raised an eyebrow. "Everything?"

Ally winked teasingly, but she seemed hurt by their discussion moments before. Had her quick dismissal of Ally's crush seemed rude?

"Is prison as bad as they make it out to be on TV?" she asked, searching for anything to make conversation.

Ally chuckled. "When it's bad, it's pretty fuckin' horrible. When it's not so bad, I guess it's just...not *ideal*." She paused. "You make family in there. Keep them close. When my parole's up, I'm going to go back and visit."

"That's really nice. I'm sure the other women will be happy to see you."

Bron caught the way Ally smirked, and she knew what it meant. "I imagine you would have been popular," she pressed.

Ally cocked an eyebrow. "And what makes you say that?"

"You're...charming. Rough around the edges, but—"

Ally nodded down to her stomach. "You mean rough around the scar tissue?"

Bron swallowed over the tightness that immediately seized her throat. "I'm sorry."

Ally swirled the inch of water at the bottom of her glass like it was vodka. "Whatever."

"Can I ask you a personal question?"

"Sure."

"Was that when you stopped volunteering? After you were burned?"

"Had to," Ally said. "I couldn't move fast enough for a long time. You know when you get a bad paper cut right on a joint of your finger? And suddenly you can't move the whole finger because you don't want to make it worse?"

"Except your finger was your entire body," Bron guessed.

Ally smiled across the swing at her. "Something like that."

"Would you go back to volunteer? You know, if you didn't have a criminal record for arson?"

"I don't think I could after getting burned the way I did," Ally said. "I'm not as fearless as I used to be."

Bron found Ally's honesty and her abandonment of pride deeply attractive.

"There are safer ways to be a hero," Ally added.

Bron shifted on the seat. "And is that what you *want?* To be a hero?"

Ally's gaze dropped to her lips. She stared blatantly, hesitating. Bron swallowed over the sudden dryness in her mouth.

"I *want*...to fuck you," Ally breathed.

Slowly, Bron shook her head. "We can't." Her throat felt like it was closing over.

"You don't want to?" Ally asked softly, the neediness in her voice entirely foreign.

Bron bit her tongue, attempting to gather her thoughts. "I need to pick up Mum and Annie."

"I could come with you," Ally suggested, standing when Bron did.

"No, I should go alone," she said quickly. "It's almost nine thirty, and after I pick them up we usually stop by the lookout for Annie to get an ice cream and Mum and I get a cup of coffee, and…We won't be back before your curfew."

"Oh." Looking for something to do, Ally awkwardly placed her hands on her hips. Her T-shirt rode up, the black waistband of her underwear completely exposed.

Bron looked away sharply. "I'm just going to grab my keys—"

"Bron, are we okay?"

"Yeah, yeah," she nodded, backing away. "Don't worry about it," she said.

"Are you sure? I didn't mean for this to be a repeat of earlier…It just came out. Being around you all the time is just making me—"

"It's fine," she said, cutting Ally off. "I really need to go."

CHAPTER EIGHT

Bron stilled Annie's bedroom door before it could squeak and wake her niece, the light sleeper. Her eyes took a moment to adjust to the semidarkness. The dim nightlight wasn't much help. She stepped farther into the room, cursing herself for forgetting to wash Annie's school uniform earlier that day.

Her gaze darted across the floor in search of the dress. Next to the bedside table were the clothes Annie had been wearing when she went to the hardware with Daniel and Ally that morning. Bron frowned at the memory of Annie swaggering into the kitchen dressed exactly like Ally had been earlier that day—denim shorts, a navy singlet, gumboots in lieu of steel-capped work boots, and her long blond hair pinned up. Annie had the whole shebang down pat. Looking between each other, all four adults had been largely amused.

A floorboard creaked under her step. She stopped and listened to the soft rustle of covers as Annie rolled over in her sleep. Bron looked to the wardrobe, remembering that she'd spotted a spare in there months ago. It was a size too big. Libby had probably picked it up at the secondhand school uniform pool shop, but Bron was fairly confident that she could do wonders with a needle, thread and duct tape.

As she moved closer to the wardrobe, she spotted the school dress in a heap around the side of the twin bed. She scowled as she picked up the uniform and, to her *absolute* delight, the pair of soaked shorts that she told Annie were to go straight into the wash after she ran around beneath the sprinkler that morning.

A glimmer under the claw-foot of the bed frame caught her eye. She peered near the end of the bed, certain of what she would find, the way it somehow caught the glow of the nightlight, before she could even examine it by touch.

It was the ring, deliberately placed under the claw-foot of the bed, out of view. Listening to Annie's gentle breathing while holding Libby's ring between her fingertips, something shifted inside of her. With the dirty clothes under her arm, she quietly closed the bedroom door. She returned to her bedroom and hid the ring beneath the paper drawer-liner at the back of her underwear drawer. *Well. There you have it. Mystery solved.*

After picking up the bathroom towels to throw into the wash, she made her way down the stairs, blinded by the huge pile in her arms. The dun-dun of a *Law and Order* rerun echoed from the lounge room before the green and blue hues glowing from the TV danced across the hallway wall. Ally was still up.

At the other end of the house, she dumped the pile of towels and Annie's dirty clothes on the laundry floor. The lid of the machine was already open. She absentmindedly dropped the uniform in first, her brain barely registering the flash of shiny, scaly brown at the bottom of the barrel before, as though possessed, the uniform rose back up, higher and higher...

Her entire body seized.

The snake hissed angrily, shaking its head to rid itself of Annie's uniform. The clink of the uniform's buttons as they hit the base of the metal tub sent a deep tremor through her.

Standing stock-still, she held the snake's gaze.

"Hey, Bron, if you're doing a load do you mind if I chuck in my—"

Ally halted in the doorway, her eyes widening as she took in the snake standing in the barrel of the washing machine.

"What do I do?"

"Okay," Ally said. She dropped the overalls in her hands and the buckles hit the tiled floor. At the sound, the snake immediately coiled its neck to appraise Ally. "Don't move," Ally whispered. "It's a brown snake."

"They're not supposed to fight," Bron argued.

"Well…"

The snake coiled itself further into an S-shape, ready to strike.

"*Don't move*," Ally repeated firmly. "It's young, so it's a lot fuckin' worse."

When it twisted back to Bron, she couldn't stop the keening noise, which etched its way desperately from her throat. "It's going to bite me." Her entire body broke out in a sweat. "Oh, Jesus. What do I do?" she rasped.

"Nothing," Ally commanded. "I'm going to hit the lid back down while it's looking at you, okay? It's going to fall straight back into the tub." Slowly, she inched closer. "Then we'll call WIRES."

The snake hissed at her again. It was *fuming*. She choked on a whimper. "Ally, don't hit the lid. It's gonna jump at me."

Ally moved closer to the lid. "It's not."

"It is, it is." The snake reared its head, its bright fangs evident. "Ally, please, don't—"

"Just shut up," Ally snapped. "Shut. Up."

The very moment Ally reached forward for the lid, the snake made to jump. But Ally was too quick, knocking the reptile back into its newfound home and out of sight. Her hands pressed tightly against the lid of the machine. "See?" she said knowingly, but the slight tremble in her voice reached Bron's ears.

Inside the machine, the snake thrashed around. The two women stood listening to the metallic thump, thump, thump, attempting to regulate their breathing.

Bron's heartbeat slowed. She cupped a hand to her lips and released a deep, shuddering breath. "Thank you," she husked.

Swallowing, Ally nodded. "We'll call WIRES in the morning."

"No, we need to call them now. It can get out through the drain hose or into the body of the machine."

"Honey, WIRES isn't gonna come out here at midnight just because we've got a snake in the tub…"

"But it's a brown snake!"

"You think you're the first person in the mountains who's had a brown snake in the house?"

She scowled, but Ally was right.

"We'll lock the laundry door. If it gets out of the machine somehow, it won't be able to get into the kitchen. It'll just go out the back."

Bron sighed. "Okay."

"Okay?"

"Fine. But Annie absolutely cannot find out."

* * *

"What's that man here for?"

Bron looked up from the fridge. Annie stood by the back screen door in her unwashed uniform, retrieved from the tub just twenty minutes before. Outside, the WIRES volunteer stood by his truck talking to Daniel.

"He was looking at the washing machine," she said casually.

Annie reached for the bowl of cereal Bron had prepared for her. "Why's he here so early?"

Worriedly, Jackie looked over the top of the newspaper.

"He's a repairman. We need a new part for it," Bron lied.

"Oh," Annie said. "Did we need wires?"

"What do you mean?" Bron asked. *How does she know?*

"His van says wires on the side. Did he bring us wire?"

She looked out the window, catching on. *Phew.* "No, no, he was fixing wires in the washing machine," she said, relieved that Annie had no idea just what the 'Wildlife Information, Rescue and Education Service' did. "Why don't you go eat your cornflakes while you watch cartoons?"

Annie looked up. "Serious? I can take my breakfast into the lounge room?"

"Don't spill."

"Promise," Annie muttered, her attention completely focused on not splashing the milk over the rim of the bowl as she made her way out of the room.

"Hey, baby," Ally muttered as she passed Annie in the doorway.

"Watch out, Al," Annie said, her tongue poking out between her lips in concentration. "Can't spill…"

When Annie was gone, Ally turned to Bron and Jackie. "Is it taken care of?"

Bron nodded. "It stayed in there all night, thank God. Kept the uniform company."

Jackie shook her head. "Sending the poor little girl to school in an unwashed uniform. You should make her wear that other one hanging in her cupboard. Or better yet, you should have let me wash it when I offered on Friday night."

"Well, Mother, if I'd remembered that I'd tossed the uniform in with the snake *before* I woke up this morning, I would have had time to adjust the spare uniform, wouldn't I? I had worse things, like, I don't know, *vengeful brown snakes* to lose sleep over last night. The uniform was the least of my problems. Besides, it's not even dirty. Wearing an unwashed uniform for one day won't kill her."

"I don't know, Bron. It was pretty crushed," Ally stirred. "She's really going to look like little orphan Annie."

Bron raised an eyebrow. *Not funny.*

"It's a joke," Ally drawled, chuckling as she dunked a tea bag into her mug. "Relax."

Jackie piped up. "Speaking of clothes." She looked at Bron. "You need to go through Libby's stuff and see what Annie would like to keep. I can call the Salvos to pick up the rest."

Bron shook her head, shuddering at the idea of Libby's clothes hanging on a rack in some cluttered Salvation Army store. "I'm not ready, Mum. I'll do it when I come back from Boston."

Jackie sighed. "Bron—"
"Mum. Not yet, okay? When I come home."

Monday afternoon brought a sweltering, stuffy heat to the Blue Mountains. The sun had such a bite to it that Bron deemed it too hot for Annie to be outside running around under the sprinkler. She would rather have a stir-crazy six-year-old on her hands than spend the night rubbing aloe vera gel into Annie's red-raw alabaster skin while she whimpered from heatstroke.

"I'm just so bored, you know?" Annie repeatedly sighed all through dinner, pushing the peas around on her plate and digging caves into her mashed potatoes. When Ally suggested they take a walk down to Echo Point for ice cream, Bron quickly agreed.

It was just the three of them. Jackie had gone over to the bowling club for dinner with friends to escape the heatwave and Daniel had fallen asleep on the lounge immediately after dinner. Bron was amazed at his work ethic. The mercury had risen over 104 degrees—no, *forty degrees Celsius*—and Daniel had spent the hottest part of the day perched on top of a ladder under the fiery sun painting the eaves of a two-story house, his neck craned back like Michelangelo. Not once had he complained, Ally told Bron as they reached the platform overlooking the Three Sisters.

Perhaps it was because her hair was still damp from her shower after dinner, but Bron thought it seemed cooler down at the lookout. Only a few tourists were on the platform, their cameras and travel backpacks giving them away. She assumed they belonged to the crowd further up the street standing near the bus parked outside the tourist centre. The ice cream shop and café inside the centre would be busier than usual.

Ally rested her elbows on the railing. Too short to do the same, Annie looked between the wide bars.

The three golden rock faces standing in darkness was a breathtaking sight.

"Do you know they all have names, Annie?" Ally asked.

Annie looked up. "What are their names?"

Next to Annie, Bron leaned against the railing, the iron still warm an hour after sunset.

Ally pointed to the left rock. "Well that one is Meehni, and the middle one is Wimlah, and the one on the other side is Gunnedoo. They're all sisters."

"Why do they have weird names?" Annie said.

Bron was about to interject but Ally spoke up. "Well, they belong to the Aboriginal legend, so their names are very beautiful."

"Oh," Annie said. "What's a legend?"

"A legend is like a made up story. The made-up story is that these rocks used to be people."

Annie raised an eyebrow. "Like humans?"

"Yep. The three sisters were from Katoomba—"

"I'm from Katoomba," Annie interrupted.

"I know you are. Anyway, the sisters wanted to marry three brothers from another tribe—a tribe is another group of people—but marriage wasn't allowed."

Annie looked puzzled. "Why not?"

"Because that was the rule. The girls couldn't marry outside of their tribe. Anyway, the brothers got really mad and kidnapped the girls. There was a big fight between the two groups. While the fight was happening, a witch doctor turned the girls to stone—just for a little while—to protect them. But the witch doctor got hurt in the battle and he died. And nobody else could turn the girls back. So they stayed like this forever."

Annie clicked her tongue. "That's not real is it?" she asked, sounding so much like Libby.

"It's not real," Bron inserted. It wasn't even entirely correct, but she decided not to tell Annie and Ally that the story was fabricated as an 'Aboriginal legend'—by a *white* local—to attract tourists.

Annie turned to Ally. "You and Aunty Bron and my mum were like sisters," she said with great certainty.

Ally bit her bottom lip for a moment before she replied. "Yeah, a little bit."

"Like the Three Sisters," Annie confirmed.

Bron and Ally were quiet.

"You two should marry brothers from another tribe and then you'll be just like the story."

Bron's gaze darted to the top of Annie's head, and then at Ally, who was looking at Bron, her lips twisted in amusement. "No, Annie," Bron said gently. "Remember when I first came home and we had a talk about how I like girls, not boys?"

"Oh, yeah," Annie said vaguely. "I forgot." She paused. "Then you should marry a lady from another tribe. Or you could just marry Ally if you can't find a different lady 'cause Ally likes girls too."

Ally slowly turned her head and looked across the railing at Bron. Her eyes were bright and vivacious, but Bron saw something else in that stare. Something more. Her eyes dropped to Ally's full lips. *I want to fuck you.* Bron swallowed. The admission had played over and over in her mind all week, distracting her, terrifying her, thrilling her...

"Ow," Annie murmured, slapping her upper arm. "A bloody mozzie got me! Can we go and get ice cream, please?"

Bron was right. The line outside the ice creamery was at least five people deep on three separate queues.

"Why don't you two go and grab a table, and I'll get in line?" Ally offered.

After giving Ally detailed instruction on exactly what cone and type of ice cream she wanted, Annie crossed the ice creamery into the adjoining café and sat down next to Bron.

"It's nice and cool in here, isn't it?" Bron asked.

Annie nodded, reaching for the end of her plait. "When we get home, can you do a fishtail in my hair just like yours?"

Bron pushed a golden ringlet behind Annie's ear. "Sure. Hey, Ann..." she said softly.

"Yeah?" She reached for a napkin and began to fold it into a paper plane.

"I found your mum's ring in your room last night when I was looking for your uniform."

"Oh."

Bron hesitated, her fingers stilling in Annie's hair. "I'm a little bit worried that Nanna might go and vacuum it up. So how about I keep it safe until you're older?"

"Okay," Annie said, discarding the half-finished plane and looking across the café for Ally.

"Anytime you want to see it, anytime at all, you just come and ask me, okay? Annie, are you listening?"

Annie refocused her attention on Bron. "I'm real sorry that I took it from your jewellery box," she said simply.

She smiled. "That's okay, sweetheart." She picked up Annie's delicate hand and lightly shook her middle finger. "When you're a big girl, that ring is going to go right here on this little finger."

Annie looked sceptical. "You really think it will fit me one day?"

"I'm absolutely sure of it."

CHAPTER NINE

"Can I borrow something?"

Bron dropped the school socks she was folding into the top drawer of Annie's dresser and raised an eyebrow at Ally.

Hovering in the doorway of Annie's room, Ally clicked her tongue. "I need something to cover this." She ran a hand over her tattooed bicep, left bare in just a singlet.

Bron grinned, pushing the heavy drawer closed. "Well, I must say, I never thought the day would come…"

"Yeah, okay, Bron. Rub it in. So have you got something I can wear or not?"

It was difficult to overlook how tense Ally seemed at the prospect of visiting her own mother. It had been Jackie's suggestion to schedule the visit to the nursing home before lunchtime that Saturday morning. Typically, Jackie said, people with dementia were more coherent earlier in the day. And while the morning hours may have been better for Kerrie, it was evidently at Ally's expense. The dark circles beneath her eyes revealed she'd either had a restless sleep or hadn't slept at all.

Bron couldn't help but wonder why Ally was so anxious. Kerrie Shepherd had always been nothing more than a caricature of the ignorant Australian redneck. Of course, to Ally, her only child, Kerrie Shepherd was multifaceted.

Ally followed Bron into her bedroom. She opened her wardrobe doors, scanning over the hanging shirts for one that would fit Ally's taller frame. She could feel the warmth of Ally's body right behind her.

"Geez, Bron, for someone who lives in another country, and for a lesbian, you've got a lot of clothes."

Bron rolled her eyes playfully, pulling out a grey plaid print and handing it to Ally. "This might work. You'll have to roll up the sleeves since the arms will be too short." She shut the cupboard doors. "Will you be too hot in this?"

Ally winked. She shrugged the shirt on over her loose black singlet top. "I don't know, will I?" she teased.

Bron chuckled and Ally looked at herself in the full-length mirror. "Good," she muttered. Bron took it upon herself to translate her approval into a 'thank you.'

"Knew you'd have something dykey."

Bron fought back a grin.

"Are you sure you want to come?" Ally asked. "I can just go with Jacks."

"What would I do here? Daniel and Annie won't be back from the footy for another few hours, and I don't have any immediate work to do. Besides we're still going to lunch afterward, right?"

Ally nodded tensely. "Right. Well…thanks."

She smiled softly. "You're welcome."

Jackie sat in the front seat for the drive to give Bron directions to the nursing home. Bron spared a quick glance up at the rear vision mirror as she turned out of their driveway and saw that Ally was already lost in a daze.

They were lucky enough to find street parking just a few blocks up from the nursing home. As the three women began the walk down the hill, Ally asked, "Which wing is she in again?"

Bron took out her wallet. In the tightest insert of her wallet was the tiny, folded piece of paper she'd found in Libby's wallet. In Libby's handwriting was the name of the nursing home and, presumably, Ally's mother's room number in the Oleander Wing.

As they walked, Ally leaned over Bron's shoulder. She read the note and nodded. Bron tucked the slip of paper back inside her wallet. Earlier that week, she'd copied the details in her own messy scrawl and given it to Ally. Not for the first time, it occurred to her that she could have given Libby's note to Ally, but she couldn't part with any scrap of paper inked in Libby's gorgeous handwriting—not to-do lists, or to-read lists, and especially not shopping lists. In Libby's script, milk, onions, zucchini and tomato sauce were more poetic than Wordsworth.

Ally broke through her thoughts. "Isn't oleander poisonous?" she asked, and then, after a moment, whispered, "Figures."

Bron faintly remembered Kerrie Shepherd. On one of her early visits home, months after Ally's father died, Bron had been driving from somewhere and passed the motel. Kerrie had been out on the balcony of the second floor of the motel, puffing away on a cigarette. Bron had slowed, almost to a stop, and waved. There was no way Kerrie couldn't have seen her. Still, she hadn't waved back, and the handful of times Bron had met her in person back in the nineties, she'd never been particularly outgoing.

"Ally's mum's not the full quid," Libby had said each time she came home from a sleepover at the motel Kerrie Shepherd owned and managed.

"Well, she's had a lot of crap handed to her, Libby," Jackie had always excused, not wanting to speak ill of Ally's mother in front of pre-teen Libby.

Much older than Libby, Bron knew back then that Jackie thought the same. Kerrie had known Jackie well enough to acknowledge her in the street, but a curt, passing hello to Jackie, who virtually raised Ally every other weekend, made Kerrie not just a stranger to their family, but strange.

Jackie signed them in at the front desk and got directions to the Oleander Wing. When they passed through the second set of glass doors, Ally exhaled nervously. Something inside of Bron urged her to reach for Ally's hand or to run a hand over her back, or to at least gently squeeze Ally's upper arm. Bron knew it was what Libby would have done for Ally, how she would have reassured her best friend. But Bron wasn't touchy-feely like Libby had been. That kind of friendly affection just didn't come naturally to her, so she crossed her arms and turned right at the rec room after Jackie and Ally.

The Oleander Wing smelled distinctly of disinfectant, but it was kind to the senses, like the nursing home staff were cleaning in preparation for dinner guests rather than disinfecting bed pans and mopping up juice spills. The door to Room 43 was wide open. Jackie stepped in first and Bron followed, Ally falling behind her.

A woman who was unmistakably Kerrie Shepherd sat in a padded chair in the corner, her eyes trained on a morning television program. Bron glanced around the room. The only suggestion that it was a nursing home suite and not a regular bedroom were the heavy white hospital curtains and the duress buttons on the walls. The bed was draped with a crocheted blanket of pastel squares. The small television sat upon a glass cabinet filled with ornaments. On a low table beneath the window sat a vase of imitation roses, framed by two photos— one of Ally's father and the other of three children, Ally's cousin's children, Bron assumed.

When Kerrie finally drew her eyes away from the TV and looked up at the three women standing in the doorway, her struggle to match memory to faces was blatantly unapologetic. "Good morning," she said. When she forced a smile, her face seemed gaunter.

Jackie was the first to move forward. "Hello, I'm Jackie." She grinned and pointed out the window. "Beautiful day today, isn't it?"

Kerrie looked away from the television and outside the sliding glass door to a small rotunda in the sunshine. "It is at the moment," she murmured. "It's going to rain later."

Jackie hummed her disagreement. "I don't know about that, but we could do with some rain, couldn't we?"

Disinterested in Jackie, Kerrie looked to Bron, who smiled warmly and moved closer. "I'm Bron." After placing a kiss into the hollow of Kerrie's wrinkled cheek, Bron turned, inviting Ally to do the same. But Ally stood back, her hands still encased in her pockets.

It didn't matter. Kerrie's attention was focused on Bron and only Bron. She looked up at Jackie. "Isn't she pretty?" she whispered to Jackie.

Jackie smiled, but looked to Ally, urging her forward.

Ally shifted closer. "Hi Kerrie."

Finally realising there were three guests in the room rather than two, Kerrie looked Ally over. She smiled at her for a moment, but her gaze shifted, lost and unsure. When she looked back to Jackie, sudden recognition washed over Kerrie's features. "You're Libby's mother."

"Yes." Jackie's eyes widened. "I am."

"Where's Libby?" Kerrie wondered.

Without sparing a glance at Bron and Ally, Jackie explained, "Libby's at home."

"I wish she'd come with you," Kerrie whined. She looked to the fabric roses on the table. "Last week she bought me those flowers."

Jackie sat down on the edge of the bed. She smoothed a hand over the blanket. "That's lovely."

Bron met Ally's troubled stare. She tried to imagine the thoughts racing through Ally's mind. It would be devastating to see Jackie like this, so ambivalent and vacant. However cruel and distant Kerrie had been in the past, she was still Ally's mother.

An elderly resident passed the doorway with a nurse, the two chatting away as the patient clicked her walker across the linoleum. They didn't spare a glance inside Kerrie's room, but Kerrie looked past Ally, scrutinizing the patient and nurse. She nodded in the direction of the open doorway. A scowl crossed her face. "She won't leave me alone. I don't know what she's up to!"

Her vision fell to the forefront, realizing Ally was blocking her view of the corridor. "What did you say your name was?"

Ally introduced herself, but Kerrie only squinted, perplexed. "What a lovely blouse," she said.

Ally's voice was gravelly when she replied. "Thanks."

Kerrie looked back at the TV, suddenly deeply invested in an infomercial for a vacuum.

"We can just go," Ally said softly.

Bron was about to argue that they'd barely been there three minutes when the nurse from the corridor knocked on the open door.

"Looks like you have some visitors, Kez," she said, her hands finding her hips. Bron guessed the nurse was wondering who they were in relation to Kerrie, but Bron didn't think it was her place to identify Ally. The nurse offered a smile to them, but Kerrie didn't look up from the TV.

"Well," the nurse said, "just letting you know that you're all welcome to join us in the rec room for morning tea."

"Thanks," Jackie and Bron said in unison.

The nurse leaned against the doorframe. "Your niece should be here soon, Kerrie."

Immediately, Kerrie reached for the television remote. As she stood, Jackie and Bron stepped back to make way for her. "There aren't many seats in the rec room, so I don't think you should come to morning tea," she said pointedly.

The nurse made a disgruntled sound of objection. "There are plenty of seats, Kerrie."

But Kerrie had already picked up her reading glasses and a Mills and Boon novel and was on her way out the door without so much as a good-bye.

"Kez," the nurse berated, clicking her tongue as she watched Kerrie walk away. "Maybe you could wait until her niece gets here," she suggested. "She's a lot better when the kids are here. It's a healthy distraction for her on her bad days."

Bron looked to Ally, already knowing what her answer would be.

"I think we'll go," Ally told the nurse. "Thanks anyway."

Resigned to the fact that she wasn't going to be able to convince Ally to wait for her cousin to arrive, Jackie excused herself to use the restroom before they left to go to lunch. Bron found herself oddly relieved to have a moment alone with Ally outside the nursing home while they waited for Jackie.

"Are you okay?" Bron asked.

Ally shrugged. She looked down at Bron. "It could have been much worse."

Bron shifted her handbag on her shoulder, the leather already sticking to her skin in the heat.

"I'm sorry that we came all this way for only a short time."

"You can't help it. It's just one of those things," Bron assured her.

"I suppose. I'd stay but…It's just that my cousin really has it in for me. She's pretty bitter, acts like she's the one putting Mum through aged care and I haven't sent a penny. Thing is, I know the money Mum made when she sold the motel is what's paying for all of this, not my cousin. The profits are probably paying for Uncle Rob's rent for this place too."

"Your uncle lives here too?"

Ally nodded. "He never liked me. None of them do." She scuffed the toe of her work boot against the garden path. "Anyway, I don't care. They can have the money, and they can think what they want about me."

Bron sighed. "I'm sorry that your family situation is shitty, Al."

Ally's smile was tight-lipped. "It is what it is. Mum and I were never close. But it does make me feel good when I think that Libby came to see her. Even if it was just once or twice."

Bron nodded. "She was a good girl, our Libby."

Ally looked down at Bron.

"What?" Bron arched an eyebrow.

"Sometimes," Ally started with a quiet chuckle, "you and Annie sound just like her."

The computer Jackie kept in the small office downstairs was hardly ever touched since Bron and Daniel each owned laptops. Annie used the outdated desktop computer once a week—under sufferance—to access her online 'Mathletics' homework, but for the most part, it remained relatively unused until Ally came along.

When she'd first arrived home from Oberon, Ally regularly used the computer to email her parole officer, and although she never mentioned it, Bron figured she must have been logging on to access her Centrelink records and payments too.

A week before, searching for an accidentally deleted file for Annie in the recycle bin folder, Bron had stumbled upon a Centrelink icon. She guessed that, not completely Internet-savvy after having been in prison without Internet access for so many years, Ally had inadvertently downloaded the Centrelink shortcut and then deleted it, too embarrassed to leave it up on the desktop for everybody to see. But what other option did Ally have but to take government handouts for the next few months until she got back on her feet? Ally had nothing to be ashamed of, but clearly she was.

"There won't be any more letters—or handouts—from Centrelink," Ally had declared at breakfast the day after Bron found the icon in the recycle bin. "So don't worry if you don't see any arrive in the mail," she added, as though they had all been eagerly awaiting the letters.

Daniel and Bron had looked at each other across the table. Jackie had been the one to speak up. "Did you go and cut them off?" she'd asked pointedly.

"Yep," Ally had said smugly. "No more handouts for Ally Shepherd."

So when Bron found Ally on the computer in the office after everybody had gone to bed, she wondered what Ally was doing.

"Sorry," Bron said. "Annie's getting her chicken pox vaccine at school tomorrow and I just need to fill out her immunization history." She waved the form in her hand. "Mum said that Libby kept Annie's baby book somewhere in here."

"No, you're all right." Ally clicked at the computer mouse a few times, obviously closing whatever she had been researching. "I'm done anyway."

Bron opened one of the desk drawers, flicking through paperwork and files in search of the baby book. "Internet working?"

"I guess," Ally murmured distractedly, standing. "I wasn't using the net."

"Oh?"

"Actually, I was wondering if you could read over something for me," Ally asked timidly. "I've written an application letter."

Ah, there you are! Bron pulled the blue baby book from the second drawer. "What are you applying for?"

Ally leaned against the bookcase full of photo albums. "There's this business course at the University of New South Wales…"

"New South…" Bron trailed off. "That's far. Is training it into the city every day something that you would be okay with?"

"It's pretty much completely online," Ally explained. Looking to her bare feet against the floorboard, she licked her lips. "My tutor at Oberon said I'd be really good for it. She reckons I could get in if I wrote a real good application letter. Plus, I can defer the cost to Study Assist until I can pay it off," she added.

Bron smiled. "I didn't know you were interested in business."

"I am," Ally said, confidence returning to her tone. "I've got a few ideas, just stuff I've been mucking around with. You know, *How to Make Friends and Get Your Shit Together.*"

Bron laughed softly.

"So could you read over the letter?"

"Oh, yeah, of course," Bron said, hoping her smile would alleviate some of Ally's newfound nervousness.

"No rush. The closing date isn't for a few weeks. I know you're busy with real work," she rambled. "Anyway, it's on the computer…"

Bron smiled. "I'll get to it as soon as I can," she said to a grateful Ally.

But her curiosity was so strong, she read over it as soon as Ally left the office. It wasn't quite a full page. Ally had detailed her educational experience, explained her time at Oberon, and described her full-time position working with Daniel as a reformed individual. The letter read eloquently and articulately.

After locking up downstairs and checking on her sleeping niece, she knocked softly on Ally's bedroom door.

"Come in," she heard faintly.

She slowly opened the bedroom door, surprised to find Ally sitting up in bed with a novel. She briefly glanced around Libby's old room. A fresh set of work clothes lay over the chair in the corner, and Libby's dresser was sparsely decorated with Ally's things—a can of deodorant, a hairbrush and her toiletries bag.

Bron focused on Ally. "I just read your letter."

"Was it okay?" Ally whispered.

"It's great, Al."

Her eyes lit up. She closed her book and sat forward. "Really?"

"Yeah. You're good with words."

"Any criticisms?"

She thought about it. "Maybe you could include some of your business ideas? It could be a draw card…"

She nodded slowly. A smirk slowly broke out on her lips. "Like the reformed prisoner draw card?"

She shrugged, a matching grin tugging at her lips. "Why the hell not?"

CHAPTER TEN

Bron hadn't realized just how much effort she'd put into Ally's birthday dinner until Jackie pointed it out at five o'clock on the fifth of December.

"Do you need a freezer bag to take the cake over to the restaurant tonight, love?" Jackie asked from across the backyard where she was down on her hands and knees, turning over the garden bed with a spade.

Bron pinned the last sock to the clothesline. "No, I already dropped it off at Lucido's before I picked up Annie from school. Did I tell you they spelled Al's name with an 'ie' on the plaque? I got all the way home this morning, opened the box to take a look, and then had to drive all the way back."

Jackie dug the spade into the dry bed of lettuce. She pushed her sunhat back from her face and wiped at her forehead. "That's a lot of trouble that you've gone to for Ally. You wouldn't have done all of this two months ago, would you? And Lucido's? That place is expensive. I thought we were going out for Chinese?"

Bron could sense what was coming, and she didn't want to have the conversation with her mother. She pulled the empty washing basket against her hip. "It's not *that* expensive. We went to Lucido's for your birthday," she huffed. She pulled a fresh towel from the clothesline, tossed it over her shoulder and disappeared upstairs to take a quick shower before dinner.

She flicked off the hair dryer, deciding to leave her hair out for once. The day had been cooler, and the temperature was predicted to drop around nine. She dabbed perfume to her wrists, remembering how Rae had been allergic to it. If there was a consolation to their breakup—and, in hindsight, there were many consolations—at least she could wear as much perfume as she wanted. Winding the cord around the handle of the hair dryer, Bron examined her reflection. *I should moisturize more. And start wearing sunscreen every day. Libby wore sunscreen every day, and her skin was gorgeous.*

Guessing Annie was more preoccupied with the toys she'd insisted on taking into the shower rather than actually washing her hair, Bron stepped out of her room to reinstate her seven-minute-shower rule. When she pulled open her bedroom door, Ally was heaving herself up the stairs.

She paused at the top step. She looked tired and sweaty, and her legs were speckled with paint. But she looked up at Bron and smiled, genuine and warm, as though coming home to her had made up for a long and tiresome day.

"I didn't hear you pull up," Bron said, pushing her hair behind her ears. "How was work?"

Ally chuckled and ran a hand over her head. "Exhausting."

"I'm sorry I missed you this morning. I didn't get to say happy birthday."

Ally shrugged. "Annie made me birthday cereal, so that made up for it." She winked. "It was nice and soggy by the time I made it downstairs."

Bron grinned. "Well, happy birthday…"

"Thanks."

Ally was staring at her so attentively that she felt colour rise to her neck. "We have reservations for seven," she said.

Ally rested her chin on the landing post, looking her up and down. "Seven people, or seven o'clock?" she asked coyly. Just as Bron was about to clarify, Ally said, "You look nice."

She glanced down, as though she'd forgotten she'd chosen the green sundress, sat on her bed and strapped her wedge heels on moments before leaving her room. "Thank you," she said. "And seven o'clock."

"I'll just have a quick shower and then I'll be down," Ally said, heading to the end of the hall.

"Annie's in there," Bron said. "But the water's been running for over ten minutes, so I don't know what she's up to."

Ally knocked loudly, grinning at Bron. "Ann?"

The water turned off. A moment later, the bathroom door opened and Annie came out, one of the thick burgundy towels wrapped around her body, so large it fell to her ankles. "You always gotta knock or else you might see me naked!" Annie exclaimed.

Ally shot a glance at Bron, smirking. Her cheeks warmed at the memory of walking in on Ally weeks before.

"Come on," Bron ushered Annie out of the bathroom doorway. "Let's get you dressed and your hair dried, missy moo."

Annie stood in the doorway, unmoving. "Are you wearing perfume?" she asked Bron.

As Ally stepped around Annie and into the bathroom, Bron felt Ally's eyes on her. A small wrinkle marred Ally's brow as her stare lingered at the curve of Bron's waist. Her raw, visceral attraction was electrifying. Bron was well aware—too aware—that her reaction to Ally's attention was so powerful because she wanted Ally too. *Perhaps almost as much as she claims to want me.*

"Ann, come out so Ally can shower."

"I'm not wearing a ponytail tonight," Annie insisted, almost tripping over the towel as Bron led her down the hall.

"No ponytail."

It wasn't until they reached Annie's bedroom that Bron actually heard the bathroom door click shut.

"You're going to love it here," Annie told Ally as the two walked hand in hand toward the restaurant. Bron thought Ally looked gorgeous in her tight, dark jeans and a new white button-up shirt, but it was the sight of her closeness to Annie that was most beautiful. "They give you dough at your table," Annie explained, "and you can make any shape you want. Monster. Princess. It's really up to you. Just don't eat the dough after they cook it because you've been playing with it and that is just *gross*."

"Do you like the balloons?" Annie asked eagerly when the waitress led them to their table. "It was my idea. Aunty Bron and I got them from Big W before I went to school today. Bet you didn't know that! I made Aunt Bron get blue because I know that's your favourite colour like me."

When they were all seated, the young waitress placed a wineglass in front of Jackie, Bron, Ally, Daniel and Carly. "We'll just be needing four," Ally said coolly, handing hers back. She looked across the table at Bron. "Even a birthday drink isn't worth breaching parole," she joked.

Bron had decided earlier in the day that, because it was a party, she would allow Annie a glass of lemonade soft drink. It was the one thing Libby had always been rigorous about. But when the table water arrived, Ally filled a glass for herself and then another for Annie. Listening to Carly's tale about a train trip from hell, in her peripheral vision, Ally slid the glass across the table to a stop in front of Annie. Annie's little hands stilled on her small lump of dough, clearly contemplating whether to accept the glass of water, or try her luck asking Bron if she could order a lemonade. Knowing that Bron was listening to Carly and, well-mannered enough not to interrupt, Annie turned her attention back to her floury creation. *Nice move, Al.* It was becoming increasingly apparent to her that Ally was not only a good influence on Annie, but a good parent.

After the pizza arrived, Annie's tiny hand cupped the shell of Bron's ear. "Can I give Ally my present now?" The gentle touch of her hand to Bron's ear coupled with the warmth of her breath spread a deep, maternal affection through Bron.

Across the table, Ally glanced up from her plate. "Hey, grub, it's rude to whisper."

Bron smiled down at Annie and pressed a kiss to her temple. "It's in my bag."

Shyly, Annie bent down beneath the table. When she stood up again, her hands were hidden behind her back.

"Close eyes," she told Ally.

Ally did as she was told. The adults watched with rapt attention as Annie positioned a box made of Popsicle sticks in Ally's cupped hands. On top of the box, Annie placed her birthday card.

"Open eyes," she said bashfully.

Bron smoothed a hand over Annie's back as she watched Ally read over the card—an A4 sheet of white paper folded in half and decorated in Annie's large, crayoned penmanship. The focus Ally gave the card, her expression devoid of any trace of condescension as she silently read over it, touched Bron deeply.

"This is really neat, Annie," Ally said, holding up the homemade trinket box. "Thank you very much! I can put my hair ties in it so they don't get lost. Come here," she said. Annie climbed down from her chair next to Bron and moved around the table to collect her thank-you kiss from Ally.

Carly and Daniel picked that moment to hand over their gift—a set of movie vouchers. "Speaking of film," Jackie said after Ally had thanked Carly and Daniel, lifting the present she had picked out with Bron earlier that week onto the table and placing it in front of Ally.

"You shouldn't have gotten me anything," Ally said. "I don't deserve it." Ally's smile and matching wink for Jackie were playful, but her words were weighted.

Jackie scoffed. "Nonsense." She motioned for Ally to look inside the bag. "That's from Bron and me."

Ally reached into the gift bag and pulled out the small black box. "You got me a camera."

"It's just a basic digital one," Bron said. "I don't know much about photography so the girl at the shop helped us pick it out, but we figured you'll get yourself a better one down the track."

Ally read over the description on the box. She looked up, first at Jackie, and then at Bron. Her gaze lingered. "Thanks so much. This is really nice. Too much, but…thanks."

Bron willed away the heat rising to her cheeks. She fumbled in her handbag for a moment, and then pushed Ally's birthday card across the table. "Happy birthday."

Grinning widely, Ally picked it up. Although the card only held some generic message inside, and all that Bron had added was *Best wishes on your special day!* and signed her name, Ally popped it into the bag with the opened cards, saving it for later. The gesture suggested receiving a separate card from Bron meant much more.

After deciding she'd consumed enough pizza to complement her surprisingly high wine intake, Bron excused herself. She felt her head rush as she flicked on the light in the small restroom and closed the door to one of the three cubicles behind her.

A moment later, the main door to the restroom clicked open. "Just washing my hands."

Ally. When Bron opened her cubicle door, Ally looked up from the sink and met her gaze in the mirror.

"Hands felt a bit greasy," Ally murmured.

"Yeah," Bron said mindlessly, trying to process the fact that Ally had actually followed her in there. She skilfully stumbled over and turned on the tap at the sink beside Ally. As the water cascaded over her own hands, she focused on Ally's. Her fingers were long and lithe. Piano hands, Bron mused.

Ally turned off the tap and dried her hands with a paper towel. "Thanks for doing all of this—dinner and stuff." She dropped the paper towel into the bin beneath the sink. "It's a lot nicer than what poor Carly got for her twenty-first."

Bron laughed, turning off the tap and accepting a paper towel from Ally who leaned back against the sink. She shifted closer, and her hip brushed against Bron's. Her tone took on an unexpected seriousness when she said, "No one's done anything this nice for me in a long time."

Bron tossed her paper towel into the bin. Acutely aware of what she was doing, she firmly pressed her lips to Ally's warm cheek. When she pulled back slightly to gauge her reaction, Ally's eyes were dark, her lips parted. Bron could feel her hot breath against her cheekbone. She swallowed harshly. The poor, shivering frequency of the radio on the windowsill danced around the bathroom, echoing a country song off the cheaply tiled floor.

Shamelessly, Ally pushed off the counter, sliding her hands down Bron's sides until they grasped her hips. The tight grip revealed her intent. Although Bron's head was spinning, she noted Ally's dilated pupils. She felt a heavy pull low in her abdomen. Emboldened by the alcohol flowing through her veins, she closed her eyes and surged forward.

Ally's lips quickly acquiesced to her kiss. When she cupped Ally's cheeks, angling her head to deepen the kiss, Ally let her revel in her newfound dominance for a prolonged moment, until Ally's growing need for control emerged. She smoothed a firm hand over the bare skin between Bron's shoulder blades, and pulled lightly at the hair at the base of Bron's neck.

When Bron's tongue slipped between Ally's lips, Ally's jaw stiffened under her fingers. Bron dropped her hands, clutching at Ally's sides. *Oh my god, she tastes so good.*

Ally withdrew her grip from the nape of Bron's neck and splayed her hand against Bron's sternum. Her fingertips grazed the base of Bron's throat and her palm was firm, almost pressing. *Is she trying to push me away?* Her mouth, hungry and hot and ardent, said otherwise.

Ally's scent was all around her. A desperate sound escaped from Bron's lips. In response, Ally wedged her more tightly against the counter. While it had been warm and comforting—albeit arousing—in Bron's ancient Toyota in the cemetery car park, this was needy and desperate. Their breasts pressed together, and she felt herself tremble as the ache between her legs throbbed at the pressure. She tried to pull herself even closer, shocked by her body's unexpected, frantic desire to articulate every bewildering thing she felt for Ally in their kiss.

The hand that wasn't at the base of Bron's neck clawed at her back, her hip, until it took an adventurous, feral descent and ran over the front of Bron's thigh, bunching up her dress as it travelled higher. She inhaled sharply at the touch. I'm wet, she thought, her tongue shying away from the touch of Ally's for a second at the realisation. But her hips pressed forward without permission. *Yes, yes.* Bron could hear her own shallow breath, the way she inhaled abruptly at the precise moment Ally gripped her between her legs, massaging that relentless pulse through the bunched material of her dress. With tightly closed eyes and a furrowed brow, she struggled to keep both feet on the floor as Ally's hand moved encouragingly.

"Al-ly," she whimpered, breaking the kiss. Her head slumped against Ally's bare shoulder, her hips pressing down against that relentless grip.

For a long moment, it continued, and Bron felt like she was soaring. But then Ally pulled back, and her hand gradually slipped away. Although Ally's chest was heaving and her rigid nipples were evident in her thin button-up, she rasped, "Not here." Still, her penetrating stare beckoned.

Wedged between the counter and Ally's torn, unmoving body, Bron fought to regulate her breathing, to calm the unsatisfied ache between her legs. She was dangerously dizzy, like when she was little and would hang her head off the back of a swing. Ally had pulled her back up too quickly, and it was going to take her a few seconds to shake off the adrenaline rush.

"Don't tell Annie," Ally grated. Her fingertips dug into Bron's side. "But that was my favourite birthday present. Ever."

Bron licked her swollen lips and ran a hand down Ally's chest. She nodded softly. Ally kissed her forehead and then she was gone.

When Bron stepped out into the restaurant corridor, their waitress was on her way out of the kitchen. "Is it okay to bring out the cake now?" she asked.

Bron nodded and returned to the table. It wasn't until after the cake arrived, they had sung "Happy Birthday," and Ally had blown out her candles, that Ally finally met her gaze for a moment as she spoke with Annie.

"What are you going to call it, Ann?" Ally asked, her eyes flickering up from Annie's cooked 'dough princess' to Bron. She looked as conflicted and tormented as Bron felt. Knowingly, she lifted the bottle of table water to Bron's wineglass and filled it almost to the brim, the instruction obvious. Annie's extensive reply fell on deaf ears. Lust swirled fiercely inside of her, demanding attention she wasn't sure she could give. She immediately downed the glass of water.

It was after eleven when they finally left the restaurant. Bron realized just how inebriated she was when she stood to take care of the bill, the digits on the screen of the credit card machine swimming as she punched in her passcode. On the way home, when Annie fell asleep in the backseat of the car with her head in Bron's lap, Bron struggled not to do the same.

She unbuckled her niece, ready to carry her inside, but Ally whispered her insistence. "You're drunk, Bronwyn Lee—let me. You'll drop the poor kid."

Trying her best not to wake Annie, Ally carried her upstairs. Bron followed all the way, her gaze focused on the perfect, firm fit of Ally's jeans, the way her white button-up pulled tightly across her back as she climbed the stairs with Annie in her arms. Ally was powerful, and dangerous, and…exquisite. *I want to touch her. I want to feel her—everywhere.* Jackie had locked up behind them and already retired to bed. The house was about to be in dark silence. Bron's body buzzed with anticipation at the memory of Ally's gruff, tortured voice. *Not here*, she had said. *So…where? When?*

"Can I sleep in your bed tonight?" Annie suddenly asked through a yawn. "Because it's your birthday?"

Bron's hope plummeted. Ally would never—could never—deny Annie.

"Why do you need to sleep in my bed? It's my birthday, not yours."

Bron's ears pricked at the objection in Ally's voice. As playful as Ally sounded, she knew there was a seriousness to her words. She had a distinct feeling Ally hoped for the same thing, even if she wasn't completely sure what that was.

"That's okay," Annie sighed tiredly. "When it's my birthday I can come back again. I'll even make you a coupon."

With Annie in her arms, Ally stopped in Libby's bedroom doorway. She met Bron's gaze, and for a long moment, they looked between each other, unsure what to do. They didn't have much choice. Once Ally denied Annie, she'd go to Bron's bed or spend the next hour making curtain calls. It wasn't going to happen. Nodding, Ally sighed in defeat.

Bron licked her lips. "You can get her into her pyjamas by yourself?"

"Yeah," Ally whispered. "Leave her with me."

"Okay, thank you. Happy birthday. Again."

Closing her bedroom door, Bron drunkenly undressed, leaving her dress, bra and shoes in a pile on the floor. Under the cover of the thin top sheet, Bron slid a hand beneath the waistband of her panties, her fingers quickly finding that all familiar, almost forgotten rhythm. She closed her eyes and shamelessly thought about Ally Shepherd.

CHAPTER ELEVEN

"Something's burning."

Bron raised her heavy head from where it was resting on her folded arms upon the kitchen table. Annie was standing in the doorway in her pyjamas, rubbing at her drowsy eyes as they struggled to adjust to the sunlight spilling through the kitchen window. It seemed as though Ally's birthday had taken it out of the six-year-old as well.

Jackie was wringing out two thick beach towels over the kitchen sink. "The bushfires have started, lovey," she told Annie.

Ally placed a full cup of water on the table in front of Bron and dropped a Berocca into the water. The vitamin tablet fizzled to the base, colouring the water orange and promising salvation. Bron glanced up at Ally with thanks and readily brought the glass to her lips. The smoke was not helping her wine-induced headache, especially when Bron knew it wasn't simple, routine back burning.

Annie sat down at the end of the table. She released a deep sigh and sank her chin into her hand. "Are we going to Sydney again?" she asked apprehensively.

Annie was too young to remember just how awful the bushfires of 2011 had been, but Jackie and Libby's tales had clearly infused her with a deep reluctance to go to Sydney to avoid the smoke—or to evacuate. Bron had been back in Boston barely a week after spending Christmas in Australia when Libby had called to tell her about the evacuation and that they'd be staying with Jackie's sister, Carol, in Sydney for a week or so.

"I really don't want to go to Sydney," Annie said, pulling her legs underneath her on the kitchen chair. "Because *Scream Street* is on Monday at six o'clock and last time Auntie Carol stayed here she wouldn't let me watch the ABC kids channel, only the news."

Between her fingers, Bron watched Ally shake her head, grinning. "Nobody's going to Sydney at this stage. The fires aren't that bad."

Jackie shook the two wet towels one final time, and disappeared into the laundry. Annie leaned back to watch her grandmother. "What are you doing, Nanna?" she asked loudly, and then explained to Bron and Ally in a soft whisper, "She's sitting on the floor."

Jackie's voice rang back into the kitchen. "I'm putting damp towels down at the bottom of the doors so the smoke can't get in. Outside may smell like a dive bar, but I won't have our home smelling like it too."

"What's a dive bar?" Annie asked.

Bron groaned at the thought of any bar.

"Are you sick, Aunty Bron?"

Across the table, Ally smirked. Bron blinked twice. "I have a headache."

Annie's expression fell compassionately. "Do you want me to give your head a smage again?"

Bron forced a smile at Annie's offer of a massage. "No, thanks, baby." The one time she'd allowed Annie to massage a headache away, her tiny fingers had dug so firmly into Bron's skull that Bron worried she would have to see a neurosurgeon afterward to make sure Annie hadn't shifted anything out of place.

The radio on top of the fridge switched to the half-hour newsbreak. The Blue Mountains bushfires was the first report.

"Do you think they'll come close to the house?" Ally asked.

"They could. God knows they have before." Jackie dumped a few plates in the sink and they crashed loudly. She turned and her gaze fell on Bron. "I want you to do something for me."

Bron raised an eyebrow.

Jackie ran the dishtowel through her hands. "I want you to pack up all of the albums today."

"Mum, the fires aren't even close yet. And it's Saturday," she complained childishly. "*And* I've got a...headache." Ally chuckled and Bron fought a smile as she sipped her Berocca.

"I don't care if it's Saturday," Jackie exclaimed adamantly. She shook a finger in Bron's direction. "You're not taking this seriously because you haven't been here during bushfire season in over a decade. If it suddenly gets worse, we can head off and go to the city to stay with Carol and Bill, but we can't fit all of the albums in the car, not with everything else. At least take the negatives out of the back of the albums so that we can get reprints."

Bron released a heavy sigh. "I would rather pay for a hotel than stay with Carol and Bill." She hadn't seen her aunt and uncle in years, and she had no desire to do so anytime soon. "Besides, Daniel wouldn't leave the house to just let it go up in..." She trailed off, noting that Annie was watching her, listening closely. The little girl had a special gift for making a mountain out of a molehill. *Watch what you say.* "He'd want to stay," she finished. *And fight for it.*

"If it comes to being evacuated, Daniel's not staying," Jackie said adamantly. "None of us are. If worse comes to worse, I may have to go to Carol's even if we aren't evacuated. If I stay here with my asthma the way it is, I'll go through that whole bloody puffer in a day."

"Well," Bron decided, "you can go to Carol's, but I'm staying here until we're evacuated."

"Um," Ally started. "I can't exactly leave here unless we're *actually* evacuated."

Bron looked to Ally. The thought of the parole agreement hadn't even occurred to her.

"Well, darl, we'll figure it out when the time comes," Jackie decided. She turned back to Bron. "Can you just do the albums for me? I don't want things to take a catastrophic turn again. Last time we just had to go…" She faltered, starting to get teary. "There are so many photos. Not to mention the framed ones."

Bron swallowed over the growing lump in her throat. She hadn't realised Jackie was so stressed about the albums. "Later today, okay? I've got a new page to start for the book, but as soon as I'm on track with it, I'll get onto the photos." Standing, she placed her glass in the sink and pressed a kiss to her mother's temple. "Don't worry so much. It'll all work out."

* * *

"Forty years old and you're still doing what your mother asks."

At the sound of Ally's voice, Bron looked up from the photo album opened in her lap. Ally shoved her hands into her pockets and looked down at her.

She shifted, realizing she'd been sitting on the floor of the office for so long that she'd almost lost feeling in her legs. She tried on her poker face. "I'm not forty. I'm thirty-eight."

Ally clicked her tongue in disbelief. "No, you're not," she teased. "You're forty."

Bron rolled her eyes. She sighed, her gaze darting across the floor, focusing on the six—no, eight—piles of photo albums surrounding her. More than half were to go with Jackie in the Nissan if the smoke got the best of her asthma. If it came down to an evacuation, Bron would take as many albums as she could with her, but there were so many other possessions that would demand rescue too, and she could only fit so much in her Toyota. Perhaps she'd be left with no choice but to take the negatives and leave the prints behind.

Bron blinked against the afternoon sunlight streaming through the window of the office. "How was your walk down to the lookout?"

Ally sighed. "Long." She chuckled lowly, and Bron raised a questioning eyebrow. "We decided to trek it down the Grand Staircase to the Sisters, and Annie freaked out on the steps and wouldn't move. When she finally got her legs working again, she was taking about one step per minute."

"They are steep," Bron said. "I used to freak out on them too. Vertigo," she explained.

"Sure," Ally teased.

The room fell silent but for the distant sound of Annie's chattering somewhere down the hallway. Ally lingered, looking around the room.

"Do you need to use the computer?"

Ally shook her head. She crossed the room and slid down against the cool wall to sit next to Bron. Ally stretched her legs out next to Bron's. Although Bron had certainly gotten some colour in the last few weeks, the contrast between their skin tones was still stark, like snow against desert sand.

Ally peered down at the photos of Jackie's family reunion Carol had hosted back in the mid-nineties. Bron remembered the trip vividly. She'd been nineteen and in her second year of university. Libby had been twelve and begged Jackie and their father for Ally to come with them. And so all three of them— Libby, Ally and Bron, had squashed into the backseat of their father's old truck, two-year-old Daniel babbling in his car seat beside them.

"Do you remember coming to Sydney with us?" she asked.

Their shoulders brushed as Ally peered closer at the album. "Yeah, I remember."

Bron stretched her neck, following the breeze of the fan as it oscillated. It didn't help much. The office was the warmest room in the house. She could see the perspiration across her own lightly-freckled chest, between her breasts.

"Found anything fun?" Ally asked.

Bron nodded toward a small pile of albums with an A3 portfolio on top. "Some portfolios from my first years of uni. I thought I threw them out during my 'I'm completely untalented' phase. The embarrassment has since worn off. They're not that bad."

Ally elbowed her lightly. "They're probably Picassos."

"Hate to disappoint, but Picasso isn't really my illustration style," she said humbly. "Nor in my talent range."

Ally grinned. "So how many have you got left to go through?"

She motioned toward the pile next to Ally, distractedly turning another page of the album and trying not to think about how hot Ally's skin was against her own.

Ally picked up another album. "I can go through this one for you."

The controlling part of Bron urged her to reject Ally's help. She wouldn't understand the relevance of half of the photos, and Bron would end up having to do it herself anyway. But even if she would have to redo it, what was the harm of including Ally or accepting her offer of help?

"Only if you feel like it."

Ally picked up the next album. "I feel like it."

The album Ally opened was Annie's birth album. *Well that's obviously a keeper, so I won't have to go through that one later.* The first few photos were of Annie in her hospital basinet and then a few of Libby and Annie. Ally turned the page. More photos of Annie, one of Libby, and then Ally.

"Were you the first one to hold her after Libby?"

Ally shrugged. "I suppose. I was there when she was born."

Her head whipped around. "You were there for the birth?" she asked, something pulling in her chest for reasons she didn't understand.

"Yeah," Ally said softly. "Weirdest and best thing I've ever seen. And the longest. I didn't eat for like twelve hours."

She laughed. "My heart goes out to you."

The petty part of her was angry at Libby for never telling her that Ally had been at the birth. Knowing Bron would come home to support her, Libby had sworn the family to secrecy, keeping the news that Annie's father had left her two months before Annie was born under wraps. It was only after he returned when Annie was three weeks old that Bron had been told he'd gone AWOL on Libby in the first place. Apparently, another secret had been kept too. Bron wanted to be upset, but all she felt was relief—relief that someone who had loved and cared for Libby so deeply had been present when Annie was born. Besides, if she'd been told Libby planned on having Ally present for the birth, Bron probably would have talked Libby into having Jackie there with her instead.

She examined the photos of Ally holding Annie. She seemed so proud, like the newborn was her own daughter.

"She was so perfect," Ally said roughly. "Most babies just look like old men, but she was so lively. And cute." After a moment, she added, "She looked like you."

Bron turned her head to fully take in the picture of a sleeping Annie. "You think?"

"Yeah, even more than she looked like Lib," Ally chuckled. "Don't worry. I never told Libby that."

Smiling, Bron sighed. "She looks like Libby now."

Bron continued flicking through the album, anticipating finding the picture of her first meeting with Annie. But the album ended with four-day-old Annie asleep in her car seat on her first trip home, and Bron hadn't flown home until a month later.

Ally closed the album. "So should we just put this one on the Leave Behind pile?" she asked sarcastically.

Bron laughed. "Most definitely." She placed it on top of the three mammoth piles to send away with Jackie.

Ally picked up a smaller, square album. "I made this one," she said.

Bron looked over Ally's forearm as she opened it. The scrapbook was carefully put together with white bordered photos on a plain black background, a single photo to a page. The photos inside Ally's album were more artistic than those beneath the plastic slips of the other albums. Somebody who knew exactly how to use a camera had obviously taken the pictures. Ally turned the page and silence settled over them.

"I look so young," Bron said softly.

The black-and-white photo had been taken on the veranda of their house, before the beams had been painted off-white. Ally had captured her midspeech. She was seated on the veranda railing—much thinner than she ever remembered being. Her eyes were wild, her jawline prominent. Barely twenty-three.

"Look at you," Bron teased, "taking sneaky photos of me."

Ally scratched at the back of her neck. "That was just before you left."

She raised her gaze and looked at Ally. Her eyes were tinted dark as she stared reverently at the picture. Low in Bron's belly, something coiled and burned. Ally looked at the photo for a moment before her fingers fumbled to turn the page.

She couldn't help but note the difference between the way Ally looked at the next picture of fifteen-year-old Libby and how she'd looked at the picture of Bron. Ally looked down at Libby's youthful smile with that same expression that flittered across her face when Annie fell asleep at the kitchen table or when Jackie patted her on the shoulder and said something motherly—like she was seeing home and family. With Bron's photo, it was different. With Bron's photo, there were traces of longing and blatant lust in Ally's stare.

When Ally came to the end of the album, Bron told her, "I've made a rule that anything homemade goes with Mum." She placed the album on the keep pile.

"You can leave it behind," Ally offered.

Bron picked out a new album for herself and another for Ally. "No," she said simply, smiling warmly at Ally as she sat back against the wall.

A comfortable silence fell upon them as they turned pages.

"Should we talk about last night?" Ally asked softly.

When Bron looked up, Ally refused to meet her gaze, appearing deeply interested in a photo album from Jackie's school days. "I mean, you clearly enjoyed it," Ally continued. "Started it, even. But I know you'd had a bit to drink and you weren't thinking clearly." She blinked twice and Bron recognized it as a nervous tick she'd never paid much attention to until that moment. "So, yeah," Ally said, redundantly. She dropped the album next to her and pulled her legs up, resting her forearms on her knees. "I don't know where I'm going with this."

Bron licked her lips. "It wasn't just because I was drunk. I wanted it."

She was expecting a cocky grin, a lust-filled glance, *something*. But instead, Ally shifted slightly so their upper arms were no longer touching. She focused her gaze on dragging her big toe back and forth across the straight line where two floorboards met. "I know what I said in the car that day in the cemetery but…Things have changed. I'm not going to have an affair with you if that's what you're after."

Bron's chest tightened at the implication. Ally wanted more than just sex. "I'm not *after* anything," Bron said. She yearned to tell Ally she wasn't looking for just an affair either, that maybe *this* was already more, but the words caught on her tongue. She couldn't lead Ally on, not when each lascivious, tormenting fantasy of Ally that crept its way into her thoughts each night was closely followed by vivid daydreams of a new life with Annie halfway across the world. They sat quietly as Bron flicked through the rest of the album in her lap on autopilot.

Ally pointed to a photo in the album opened across her thighs. Libby was dressed warmly, standing Annie, a toddler, upright in the snow. "She wore the shit out of that jumper," Ally said, her voice still husky.

Bron pursed her lips. "I don't remember it."

"Are you kidding?"

She looked up at Ally, whose eyebrows were raised in disbelief. "You really can't remember it?" Bron instantly felt lightheaded with guilt.

"Come on, Bron." Ally laughed, her words biting. "It was like she didn't own any other clothes, and God knows that wasn't the truth. She wouldn't have chucked it. It's probably still with her stuff."

Bron's eyes watered. "Oh, I think I remember now," she managed, but she couldn't remember it. She closed the album in her own lap and stood up. "I'll be back in a sec," she rasped.

She took the stairs two at a time and went straight for her room to the rack of Libby's clothes. There it was. She was instantly blinded by the horrible yellow and orange stripes. She reefed it from its padded hanger and buried her face in it, the pulls in the wool scratching across her smooth cheeks. She sank down onto the bed, Libby's scent overwhelming her. Her tears saturated the wool of her dead sister's jumper.

Her bedroom door click closed. A sob ripped its way out of her throat as the mattress shifted with new weight. Ally pulled the jumper from her grasp and gathered Bron in her arms. "I shouldn't have made you feel bad about not remembering," Ally murmured against the top of Bron's head. "I'm sorry."

Bron's forehead pressed against the tendons in Ally's neck. "I just miss her so much," she sobbed. "If I knew she was going to die so young I never would have left. I never would have gone."

Ally wrapped her arms around Bron and held her tighter. "I know. I know," she soothed, resting her chin on the top of Bron's head.

Bron closed her eyes against the comforting sensation of Ally's fingers raking through her hair at the base of her bun.

"I feel…" Bron trailed off. *Safe. Loved. Understood. Like you're the only one who misses her like I do.*

She pulled back with a deep sigh and met Ally's gaze. Ally's hold loosened. She rubbed a thumb across Bron's tear-stained cheeks in an attempt to dry them. She examined Bron's expression so carefully, so attentively. Suddenly, Ally's lone arm around her didn't feel as comforting as it did arousing.

"Are you okay?" Ally said quietly.

From the base of the stairs, Jackie called them down for dinner.

Unmoving, she exhaled. "Al?"

Ally's gaze fell to Bron's lips while she rubbed her back. "Yeah?"

Jackie called out a second time.

"Can we finish this later?" Ally whispered.

CHAPTER TWELVE

"Can't you come too?" Annie whined.

"No."

Bron pushed the last bag of Libby's clothes—the god-awful jumper zipped inside—against the far back window of Jackie's compact Nissan. "It'll only be a few days. Three at most."

Although they hadn't received an official evacuation warning, the bushfires had flared up overnight, and Jackie's asthma had worsened as a result of the overwhelming smoke, a dirty grey blanket across the green valley. As for Annie, it made more sense for her to go with Jackie than it did for her to stay. If they were suddenly evacuated, Bron didn't want Annie to live the horror of farewelling the only home she'd ever known as it vanished through the back window of a car, left to be swallowed by flames. Annie had already experienced enough traumas for a lifetime.

In a last attempt, Annie decided to drop the 'aunt' title. "Bron, please," she tried, pressing her body against the side Jackie's car. "Can't we at least wait until Al and Dan come home from work? I don't think I said good-bye properly."

Bron sighed, her heart aching for Annie. "You said good-bye properly, I promise. And you can call and talk to them tonight, baby. They won't be back for a long time yet."

Jackie came down the front steps, keys in hand. "Now, don't forget, I've washed your sheets with Ally's," she told Bron. "They're in the dryer, so you may have to check on them. Also, let Ally know that her first phone bill is due tomorrow, and she'll need to pay it before she gets a fine! I told her getting that mobile wasn't worth it. She barely touches it! But does she listen?"

Bron nodded. "Okay, Mommie Dearest, will you get in before Little Miss has a hissy fit?"

She shuffled her reluctant niece around to the other side of the car and into the backseat. "You're going to have so much fun in the city." Annie pulled a face of disagreement. "You are," she insisted. "Nanna's going to take you to the zoo tomorrow, and you'll spend all day with the giraffes and the monkeys…" she rattled off, clicking Annie's seat belt into place. "You'll get to see the Christmas tree in Martin Place and the Christmas windows at Myer." Annie looked down at Bron's fingers pulling at the belt across her lap, assuring it was clicked in.

"Please come with us," Annie said softly.

Bron cupped her heart-shaped face in her hands. "I have to stay here with Ally and Tammy and Dan to make sure they don't get up to mischief. I love you, Annie. Be a good girl for Nanna."

Annie's little arms wrapped tightly around her neck. She pressed her lips against Bron's cheek. "I love you. And you're not so bony," she whispered. "You feel like Mummy."

Bron's heart fractured in her chest. She smoothed a hand over the back of Annie's head, her eyes watering.

"Bye, baby."

Bron craned her neck through the open driver's window to kiss Jackie's cheek. "Call me when you get to the McDonald's at the halfway point, okay?"

"Will do, love," Jackie said. "Ready to go on an adventure, Annie girl?"

As she watched the car drive away, Annie's words echoed in Bron's mind. *You feel like Mummy.* Bron remembered when

Libby had left two-month-old Annie with her to go out for a night—her first night away from the newborn for a few hours. She'd thought Libby overdramatic when she arrived home an hour and a half later, plagued with guilt.

Now, she understood.

As expected, Ally and Daniel returned just after lunch. Bron was at the kitchen table with her laptop when Ally stepped through the back door, her eyes glassy and swollen, tears rolling down her cheeks. She was stone-faced.

Bron gasped. "What happened?" In twenty-five years, she'd never seen her cry.

A ferocious grin slowly broke out over Ally's face. "Gotcha."

Utterly confused, Bron brought a hand to her heart. Ally's tears continued to roll freely.

"I'm having a reaction to the smoke."

Bron's heartbeat slowed with patent relief. "You're having a reaction to the smoke?" she clarified.

Ally swiped at her cheeks. "It's really bad down at the job we were working. It was an outside job, and it just got to my eyes. Now I think they're going to fall out," she chuckled.

Bron moved closer to examine her bloodshot eyes. Ally wasn't exaggerating. The odour of smoke on her clothes was so overpowering, Bron was surprised Ally's eyes hadn't completely dried up.

She cringed. "You've been rubbing them too."

Ally rolled her eyes at Bron's berating tone, but the gesture didn't have as much weight when her eyes were filled with tears.

"We have an eye bath upstairs," Bron said. "It's in the top drawer—"

Ally squeezed her eyes shut, utter discomfort scrunching the rest of her sharp features.

"Come on," she said. "I'll help you."

She led Ally upstairs and instructed her to perch on the edge of the bath while she fiddled in the top draw, pulling out the eyeglass. She poured a thin fountain of table salt into it and turned on the hot tap, filling it to the brim with warm water.

"Who would have thought I used to be a firey?" Ally chuckled.

"It's been a long time. Your eyes aren't used to dealing with it anymore. Head back."

She gently rested the rim of the cup at the base of Ally's left eyelid. "Don't close it," she instructed.

Ally's eye was opened wide, strained in concentration. She huffed, her breath hot on Bron's inner wrist. "I can't make any promises."

Bron tipped the cup over Ally's eye. As far as she could tell, Ally's top eyelid had stayed open. But despite the tight seal Bron had attempted, saltwater still dribbled over her cheek, running to her jaw and cascading to the bath mat.

She lowered the cup, and Ally immediately pulled back, vigorously blinking. She bent to look up into Ally's soothed eye. "Better?"

Ally tried to focus her watery left eye. "Yeah, much," she breathed after a moment. "Still tight, but less itchy. Thanks."

Bron turned back to the sink to clean the eyeglass.

"I can probably do the other eye myself," Ally offered.

"No, no, I'll help." She pinched the same amount of salt into the glass again.

The old bath creaked as Ally shifted on the rim of it. "It's so quiet. I don't know who's louder—Annie or Jackie."

Turning off the tap, Bron grinned. "Mum, probably."

She slowly turned back to Ally, careful not to spill any saltwater over the rim of the eyeglass. "Ready?"

She repeated the treatment. This time more water escaped from the lip of the plastic. As she tried to angle the cup up, the skin of her inner wrist brushed Ally's warm cheek.

She must have moved the cup into an uncomfortable position, because Ally quickly pulled back, laughing. "Geez, you're supposed to be washing out my eye, not prepping me for a lobotomy." She squeezed her eyes shut tight and rubbed at the ridge of her eye socket with her fingers.

With a wide smile, Bron ran the pad of her thumb along the ridge of Ally's wet cheekbone. Her wet eyelashes were clustered together, tiny droplets hanging from the ends like miniature crystals. Until then Bron had never noticed how long they were.

Ally stared up at Bron affectionately, her eyes red and glassy. Her fingers curled around Bron's wrist, holding Bron's touch to her cheekbone. Ally tilted her head and chastely kissed the inside of Bron's wrist. She fought against the urge to close her eyes, watching Ally's lips closely instead. When they parted against the valley of the tendons and veins in Bron's wrist, intent on a more passionate adoration, she withdrew her hand.

"Daniel's downstairs," she whispered, moving back to the sink to disinfect the eyeglass with Dettol. In the reflection of the bathroom mirror, she watched Ally run a hand through her short hair, her dark, troubled stare fixed on the ground.

"Well, thanks for the help, Nurse Bron."

Bron cleared her throat. "You're welcome."

"I'm going to go and get out of these smoky clothes before I eat," Ally murmured.

When Ally brushed past, her entire body thrilled at the contact.

Downstairs, Daniel's tall form was leaning against the kitchen counter, an all-knowing expression painted across his face. "I wondered where you two disappeared to."

Bron reached up into the cupboard for a glass. "I was helping Al wash out her eyes."

Daniel raised a thick eyebrow.

"Shut up, Daniel."

"What's going on with you and Al?" he asked.

"Sorry?"

"You know she's got it bad for you, right?"

"No, she hasn't."

"She has. She looks at you like you hung the moon, and you know it."

"Well, you're too young to remember," she started softly. "But Al had a bit of a crush on me when we were younger."

"Yeah, Mum and Lib told me." Daniel looked in the direction of the doorway. He lowered his voice. "I think it's more than a crush, though."

She tensed. "What makes you say that?"

Has Ally said something to Daniel? A wave of shame and embarrassment immediately washed over her, and she hated that she couldn't pinpoint where it came from.

Daniel shrugged. "She talks about you a lot at work, and sometimes I catch her looking at you. Stuff like that. All I'm saying is don't mess with her feelings. She might be a bit wild, but when she wants something, Ally gets real intense about it. Just be careful."

She swallowed over the dryness in her mouth. "Okay, Mum," she managed to joke.

They both looked up when Ally swung open the back door.

Daniel cleared his throat. "I think I might go over to Carly's tonight."

"She's welcome to stay here," Bron said, feeling Ally's gaze on her, watching Daniel's stare dart between the two women. She fought against the blush that began to rise at the realisation that her brother had been witness to the tension between herself and Ally for a while.

Daniel scoffed. "Yeah, nah." He stood and placed his glass in the sink. "Her parents aren't home." Ally wiggled her eyebrows at him. "Shut up," he replied. "She's all alone over there with the fires."

"Oh, please," Bron laughed. "She's not even in the danger zone!"

Daniel ignored her. "If there's an evacuation, you can just give me a ring and I'll come back and load up. And maybe, if you're lucky, I'll take you two with me."

"Surely you can fit Tammy and I in at least?" Ally joked, winking at Bron.

Daniel laughed, already halfway out the door. "Can I trust you two not to kill each other tonight?"

Bron smiled at Ally, but her features were cloaked in seriousness, as though she were lost in thought.

When her brother was gone, she turned to Ally. "I've got another page to finish, so I'm going to head back up."

Standing in the middle of the kitchen, Ally shoved her hands into her pockets, as though she was afraid she'd reach for Bron without permission. Her gaze flitted over the length of Bron's body. "Okay."

"Oh, your sheets are in the dryer," Bron said. "I would have made your bed, but I didn't want to invade your privacy."

Ally's expression may have been distracted—*anguished*—but her voice was clear and deep when she said, "You can invade my privacy."

"Are you sure your eyes are okay to eat out here?" Bron wondered. "I know it's cooler outside, but it's still pretty smoky."

Ally looked up from the porch swing. "It's really not that bad. Seems smokier inside." Thanks to a bottle of eyedrops that Bron had found in the pantry, Ally's eyes, which had gleamed a bright, bloodshot red just hours before, were almost healed.

Bron handed Ally a bowl of warm chicken salad. "The tomato is a bit how's it going," she warned.

Ally shrugged and dug her fork in hungrily. "It'll do."

As she poured herself a glass of water, Bron took in the sky. The hot westerly winds had calmed their assault on the fires, but the smoke still lingered, blanketing the setting sun.

"It's much better than last night."

"Better than earlier today too," Ally agreed. "Hopefully this is the worst of it for the year. The radio said the helitankers are flying over tonight to douse the last of the fires in the north."

"Want to walk down to the lookout to watch them fly over?" Bron wondered.

"It's forty-two degrees," Ally chuckled. "I don't want to do much of anything."

When they finished their salads, Ally sat back against the porch swing and sighed. "I wanted to have the cubby house finished for Annie by Christmas, but I've barely started."

Bron looked across the circular driveway to the timber scaffolding of a miniature house. "You've been busy with work. Why Christmas?"

Ally shrugged. "I thought it would be cute if Santa left her presents in there for her."

"That would have been cute. Maybe Santa can do that next year."

Ally's chestnut stare bore into Bron's. "That's if Annie's here next Christmas. Who knows? Her Yankee aunt may scoop her up and take her away to some foreign land."

Bron averted her gaze at the biting tone of Ally's joke. They were quiet for a long moment before Bron spoke up. "Hey," she said. "Do you remember the Christmas I came home when you were seventeen?"

Ally nodded. "Yeah."

"I was sitting out here—"

"Yeah, okay," Ally said. "I know what you're going to say, so we don't need to go over it."

Bron's lips curved up into a smile. "You know," she said lowly, imitating Ally. "I'm seventeen now, and I know what I want."

Ally scoffed. "I did not say it like that."

Bron grinned. She could vividly remember Ally's inflection, as well as the way she'd looked at Bron. "I have a pretty good memory of how it went down."

"Yeah, well, at the end of the day, nobody went down, did they?"

Laughing, Bron stretched her legs out on the seat. Ally's gaze unashamedly travelled to the line of her shorts.

"Don't be so embarrassed," Bron said. "It's not like you let it go after that."

"I thought you'd changed your mind," Ally mumbled, taking a sip from her glass. "Why else would you have offered to drive me back to the motel that night?"

"Perhaps because you were technically still a child and I was the only sober one who could take you back?"

Ally huffed. "Well, I thought it was code for 'changed my mind, let's do it in the backseat of my Toyota.'"

Bron's memory of the late night drive across town fifteen years ago was vague, but she recalled parts of it, namely the way Ally's confident hand had reached across the console and rested on her bare thigh. Seconds later, Bron had slowly unpeeled Ally's fingers from her skin. Words had not passed between them, but the sting of rejection had been as bitter as ever.

"I was pretty cocky," Ally admitted.

"Yes. You were."

Ally cleared her throat. "Well, it was worth a try."

Bron let her hair down in an attempt to conceal the flush rising up her neck.

"It may have seemed confident," Ally said softly, "but I'd been building myself up to that for a long, long time."

Bron licked her lips. "I'm sorry. I knew you had a crush on me. I could have been gentler with the way I let you down—"

Ally placed her glass down on the small table in front of them. "It wasn't a crush," she asserted. Her whole body seemed to stiffen in frustration. She ran her hands over her thighs for a moment, visibly trying to calm herself.

A company of white-feathered cockatoos swarmed in to join the pandemonium of galahs in the gumtrees over the driveway, their squawks loud and harsh.

"It's funny," Bron started. "We never really got along when Libby was around."

Ally shrugged. "Because you were jealous of me."

Bron stood, moving to splay her arms against the railing of the veranda. "Yeah," Bron confessed, hopping up to sit on the railing. "I think I was jealous. I *know* I was."

Bron looked down at Ally, her gaze calculating. When Ally met her stare, it was reluctant and brief.

Bron's jaw tightened. "Do you not want to be with me all of a sudden?" Bron said heavily. "Is that why you're so standoffish?"

"I told you that I don't want an affair."

I'm not talking about an affair and you know it. "So you don't want to be with me? That's that?"

Ally's stare, brooding and intense, revealed her desire for much more than sex. Slowly, she stood, picking up her glass and taking a long gulp of water. She moved much closer and placed the glass on the wooden railing next to Bron's thigh.

Ally planted her hands on either side of Bron's legs. "Be with you?" Ally clarified, her warm breath fanning Bron's chin. "As in fuck you?"

Bron's gaze flickered across the lines of Ally's face before she focused on her anguished stare. Her pleading eyes asked if it would mean more.

Bron nodded solemnly.

Ally raised her hands, cupping Bron's face. She pulled their mouths together, and the tense ache in Bron's chest immediately calmed as she parted Bron's ravenous lips. Humming, Bron slid one hand behind Ally's neck and arched her back.

When Ally pulled away, her lips found the underside of Bron's jaw, determined to leave a mark.

Bron's legs tightened around Ally's waist, the sound of her own heartbeat thrumming in her ears. "Touch me."

Ally groaned. "Let me take you upstairs," she rasped, planting kisses in the hollow of Bron's throat.

Dizzied by Ally's tight grip on her waist, Bron eagerly nodded her consent. Ally lifted her down from the railing, grasped her hand, and led her upstairs. As they reached the top, Bron pulled on their clasped hands, pressing her body against Ally's. As their lips met again, Ally gripped the bottom of Bron's singlet, pulling it over her head and discarding it against the hallway wall. Ally's warm hands splayed across Bron's waist, goose bumps rising upon Bron's pale skin.

Bron guided them into her room, locking the bedroom door behind her as Ally reached around her and unclasped her bra. As the thin black straps slid to Bron's elbows, Ally's palms travelled over the expanse of Bron's back, her abdomen, finally cupping her breasts. Ally groaned, gently kneading the tight flesh. When she scraped her thumbnails over Bron's nipples, Bron shuddered in her arms.

The backs of Bron's knees hit the mattress, and the familiar creak of her bedsprings reached her ears as Ally pushed a firm hand against a shoulder, urging her to lay down. Immediately, Ally straddled Bron, her lips confident, her tongue vigorous and hot as she found Bron's nipples.

Ally's mouth was relentless. When she bared her teeth against Bron's ribcage, Bron's hips pressed up of their own accord. Ally's fingers fumbled with the button and zip of Bron's denim shorts. Her hands shook as she pulled Bron's shorts over her hips, her underpants gone with them.

Ally dragged a finger from the wet, pink flesh between her legs to soft, pale breasts with their peaked tips. Her stark nakedness was suddenly more than apparent. And Ally was still completely dressed. Bron reached up in an attempt to rid Ally of her singlet, but Ally swatted her hands away.

A thrilling surge of arousal curled in Bron's belly as Ally's hot kisses crossed her waist, lower and lower until flames licked her inner thighs in the aftermath of Ally's sizzling tongue. Ally's hair tickled the insides of Bron's legs, and she opened them further, desperate with anticipation.

The second Ally's lips met Bron's core, her hips spasmed, arching into Ally's kiss. Ally groaned, deep and guttural, as her tongue worked. Bron's hips lifted from the bed, electrified by Ally's intimate caress. Ally wrapped her arms around Bron's thighs and pressed a hand to her belly, holding her against the mattress.

Fisting another tremoring hand in Ally's hair, Bron opened her eyes to watch Ally, her lips swollen and persistent. Bron whimpered at the sight. Ally's hooded gaze met Bron's, and in a quick transition, two fingers replaced Ally's mouth. She crawled up next to Bron, pushed aside her blond hair and kissed her.

Bron tightly grasped Ally's tattooed arm, her need for release, for more, increasing each time Ally curled her fingers inside. She unskilfully slithered a hand inside Ally's shorts.

Ally quaked when Bron's fingertips found wet curls. But Bron couldn't concentrate enough to please Ally properly, not when Ally's thumb was suddenly reaching higher, drawing circles against her hard, swollen flesh. Overwhelmed, Bron broke the kiss. She gasped, her eyelids shuttering.

Ally held herself up on one hand, hovering over Bron, watching intently. She curled her fingers again and again, making Bron's abdomen contract. Her thighs tightened around Ally's hand and her lips parted.

"Look at me," Ally demanded, and she immediately obeyed.

Ally's palm flattened against her core, firm and warm. Bron cried out, her body throbbing in release as she pulsed around Ally's fingers, her heartbeat slamming against her ribs. She fell against the mattress, boneless. When Ally gently withdrew her hand, she winced at the sudden emptiness. Slowly, her laboured breathing calmed.

Propped up on an elbow, Ally looked down at her, with an admiring and patient gaze. Bron smoothed her thumb across the barely-there crow's foot at the edge of Ally's eye. "You're gorgeous." Her hand travelled over Ally's jaw to the neckline of her singlet. "Take this off," she murmured.

Ally sat up and removed the navy shirt, tossing it on the bed where it landed on a pillow. The sun had almost completely set, and without any artificial light in the room, Bron strained to fully appreciate the fine details of Ally's skin and gorgeous body. Her hands sought Ally's sides, trailed them across her chest, and found that, as she had imagined, Ally's breasts were taut and firm. Even in the dim light, she could see the tattoo of Annie's name had completely healed.

Bron's gaze dropped much lower. The burn scar. It was a medal of honour that Ally would wear for the rest of her life. How many lovers had seen it or touched it? She wanted to know the details, but Ally had already unclasped her bra, and her dark nipples were begging for attention.

Bron pressed Ally down. Her lips found her right breast. Ally groaned, her fingers tracing their way into Bron's hair. Bron kissed her way across Ally's chest. When she lowered herself completely, the sensation of their bellies and breasts pressing together was devastatingly *good* and *right*.

As Bron's lips found Ally's, her knee pressed into Ally's core, against the seam of Ally's shorts. Ally sighed, her hands finding purchase on Bron's shoulder blades.

"You're all I think about," Ally said in a breath.

Bron examined her stare. She wet her lips, flushing as she tasted herself on them.

"I'm not imagining it, am I?" Ally said.

Bron was quiet so Ally squeezed her waist.

"No," Bron breathed. "I don't think so."

Ally's fingertips dug into the ridges of Bron's back, and she pushed down against her knee. She pressed a cheek against the mattress, casting her gaze to the headboard. "Oh my god, Bron. This feels so fucking good, so fucking hot…" she whispered, her voice low and cracking.

Bron had to have her.

Ally groaned when Bron pulled back, her own wetness gliding across the bare skin just above Ally's knee and leaving a trail. She ignored it, along with the hot pressure burning once more between her legs and the sweat breaking out across her skin. Wide-eyed, she hastened to get Ally's shorts and underwear down her long, smooth legs.

The wet curls at the juncture of Ally's thighs were as dark as Bron had expected. Naked against Bron's cream-colored sheets, Ally was stunning. Her body was lean, her skin smooth and flawless. The tattoos, the scar… It was all so perfectly Ally. She'd never been with a woman like her. Nobody so young, nobody with so many jagged edges, nobody who made her come the way Ally had.

Ally breathed heavily, watching Bron as she kissed Ally's abs, the scar, and lower, past those short, black curls. She hooked her legs over Bron's shoulders. Arousal twisted in Bron's belly at the sight and scent of Ally. She bent her head and timidly touched Ally with her tongue. A sigh escaped her lips. In response, Ally's thighs tensed against her ears. My god, Bron thought. *She's trembling*. Bron chanced an upward glance and found Ally's hands fisted in the sheets, her gaze on the trajectory of Bron's lips. She looked positively desperate.

CHAPTER THIRTEEN

Bron stretched across the mattress, her toes curling in the bedsheet as she watched Ally. She was standing over Bron's desk in just her underpants, inspecting Bron's most recent illustrations.

"They're not finished," she said softly.

Ally didn't turn around, allowing Bron to admire her perfectly sculpted back a moment longer. "You're so talented."

"Lots of practice."

Ally hummed her disagreement. She looked out the window above the drawing table and fixed her gaze on the clearing valley in the distance. "Looks like we packed up for nothing."

"Can you open the window?" Bron asked, suddenly feeling overwhelmed by the stifling heat of the bedroom. The fan continued to spin in the corner. She had a vague memory of Ally reaching over her to turn it on after they'd last made love, sometime after four a.m.

Ally lifted the window and wedged it open with the thin stick of wood. The morning breeze flooded into Bron's bedroom, the mild scent of scorched Blue Gum riding its wave. The cockatoos were back, loud and talkative.

Ally crossed the room and sat on the edge of the bed. She laced their fingers together. Bron's gaze travelled down Ally's front. She admired Ally's naked breasts, the dark nipples she had adored with her mouth hours before. Ally looked up from their tangled fingers and smiled hopefully at Bron.

"Daniel will be home soon," Bron said softly.

Ally's stare wandered across Bron's naked body. She pressed a hand against Bron's side, her thumb tracing the point of Bron's protruding hipbone. She leaned down and pressed a gentle kiss to Bron's collarbone before she pulled back. "I'm going to take a shower."

Bron laid there for a while, the fresh morning air cooling her warm skin. The smoke was still pungent, but it had certainly drifted north overnight, granting Katoomba a reprieve. She listened to the running water of the shower, her mind racing as she thought about Ally, and Annie, her ageing stepmother and Daniel. She would forever remember the grave expression he had worn when he picked Bron up from Sydney airport after the accident, how he had visibly swallowed when he spotted Bron coming through customs. He'd taken her directly to the funeral home to see Libby, where Bron had sat with her sister, holding her stiff, cold hand for close to an hour before she kissed Libby's forehead and said good-bye.

Bron sighed, listening as the old pipes ceased their hum the moment Ally's shower turned off. The bathroom door creaked open, and a moment later Ally was standing in Bron's doorway in a towel, her hair wet and pressed against the sides of her face.

Ally grinned, running her gaze over Bron's nakedness. "You're just an exhibitionist, aren't you?"

Bron laughed.

"If you want a shower, I'll get breakfast ready," Ally offered.

When Bron went downstairs after her shower, breakfast was only half made. Tammy was outside the laundry door, hoeing into her bowl of kibble on the veranda. Ally was peering at the toaster in a daze. She looked up when Bron stepped into her line of sight.

"Is everything okay?" Bron ran a hand over Ally's forearm.

Four slices of almost-burned toast jumped up from the toaster. Ally nodded, pinching the charred bread from the grills and dropping them on a plate. "Yeah, of course. Just in a trance."

Bron could hear the anxiety in her voice. And her tea was still black. After she added milk, it only took one tiny sip of the steaming tea to know that it was unsugared too. When Ally glanced up from buttering their toast and noticed Bron cringing at the bitter taste, she murmured an apology. Bron reached across the counter for the sugar pot. "Too distracted by thoughts of me showering to make breakfast properly?"

Ally gestured for Bron to take a slice from the plate of toast between them. "Among other things."

The unspoken acknowledgment between them manifested into a long silence.

Bron sipped at her tea and leaned back against the counter. "Can we keep this between us for a little bit longer?"

Ally paused midbite, her toast crunching. "You don't have to panic," Ally said after she had swallowed. "I'm not going to make you U-Haul."

"I thought that was just an American joke."

Ally swiped at the buttery crumbs at the side of her mouth. "Lesbian jokes are universal."

A grin broke across Bron's lips as she stared into her milky tea.

"I'm not going to say anything," Ally said. "You don't have to worry." Bron brought the cup to her lips, but before she could take a sip, Ally whispered, "I think maybe I'm more into you than you're into me."

She immediately shook her head. "Al—"

"I don't mind," Ally asserted with an expression of feigned acceptance.

She reached across the table and grasped Ally's wrist. "That's not true."

Ally's eyebrows furrowed. "Really?"

Light-headed, Bron nodded. "You know, I keep thinking that I want to tell Libby about this. About us." Bron licked her lips. "I mean, she probably wouldn't have really been into the whole idea," she added in an attempt to lighten the mood.

Ally wrapped her hands around her mug of tea. "Does it matter what Libby would have thought?" she asked seriously.

Bron contemplated the question. She supposed it didn't matter.

"Can we not talk about Libby?" Ally asked quietly. "Just for today?"

"Okay."

For what seemed like the first time in a lifetime, in broad daylight, Echo Point lookout was completely devoid of tourists. The local radio bulletin had said the cancelled coaches from Sydney to the Greater Blue Mountains would return early the next day for the busloads of visitors to admire Australia's very own emerald Grand Canyon. For now, it was just Ally, Tammy, Bron and a few locals.

The sky was overcast, gloomy with rainclouds—not smoke—for the first time in too long. Although the fires had not reached the north escarpment of the richly-green Jamison Valley where The Three Sisters stood, smoke still drifted down from further north, spoiling the eucalypt haze. The promise of rain was a godsend.

At the end of the leash, Tammy laid across Bron's sneakers, her fur coat tickling her ankles. Thankfully, with the promise of rain, the weather—and the asphalt—had cooled enough for the poor dog to be walked.

She rested her forearms upon the ledge and looked out across the valley. "It's beautiful here."

Ally nodded, crouching down to give Tammy a drink of water from the plastic bottle. "You don't realize how much you've missed it until you see it."

She considered Ally's words. *Tell her.* She inhaled deeply. "After I come home from my next trip, I don't know if I'm going back to Boston for good—with Annie."

Ally slowly stood. She twisted the cap back on the water bottle, avoiding her eyes. "You can't take her away from her family," she stressed firmly.

The assertion made Bron stiffen. "I've...I've been offered a teaching job at the Massachusetts Institute of Technology." She paused. "I don't think I can turn it down."

A line appeared between Ally's brows. "You don't think you can turn it down? What does that mean?"

Bron's heart hammered against her ribcage. "I don't know if I want to turn it down."

Ally pinched the bridge of her nose and her eyes slipped closed. "Hang on a second. When were you offered the job?"

Ship, meet iceberg. "Months ago."

"*Months* ago? Why the fuck am I only hearing about this now?" Ally snapped.

"Nobody knows," Bron said defensively. "I have to give MIT an answer by January," she added.

Ally looked up and met her gaze with a fiery stare. "If you're truly thinking about it," she continued, "you don't have my blessing. You can't do that, Bron. Libby wouldn't want that."

"What about what I want?"

Ally blinked twice, her eyes wild with disdain for the words fighting their way past Bron's lips. "It's just a job, Bron. You already have your books, your publisher. You make a mint. Why can't that be enough?"

Bron looked away from Ally's vexed gaze. "I've wanted MIT for longer than I can remember. And I have friends in Boston, a home. I made a life there."

"Really? For someone with so many friends over there, they've come up in conversation a whole three times in the past few months."

"My home is not here," Bron retorted.

Ally gripped her forearm, and Bron seized at the touch. There was suddenly so much pain in Ally's angry gaze. "Sometimes you just have to go with what life throws at you," she said bluntly. "You don't get to decide what you want anymore. If you want Annie in your life, you don't have a choice. You stay here. Make the sacrifice or give up custody and go back to Boston. Those are your options."

Bron faced her. "Contrary to the way you like to make a martyr of yourself, some of us possess the ability to make compromises."

"Say what you want, but I'm not going to bite," Ally declared, her voice gravelly. "What's the point? You already know what you want to do."

"Yeah, and what is that?"

The intensity of Ally's glare burned through her. "What are you trying to do here? Do you want me to fight you for Annie? You may have sole custody, but Annie belongs to me now just as much as she belongs to you." Ally's eyes searched her face for an answer. "Are you trying to start something with me because you just can't get over how good last night was? How good we were together?"

"No," Bron said. "Of course not." She looked away from Ally's scrutinizing gaze.

"Really?" Ally scoffed. "I know the whole Boston thing had to come up some time, but I think you're bringing it up now because you're overwhelmed. You're acting out. It's what you do."

A small lizard ran along the edge of the lookout and Tammy barked at it, turning the heads of the few locals standing nearby.

"What do you want?" Ally said lowly. "You want me to beg you to stay?"

Angered by the accuracy of Ally's assumptions, Bron shook her head and tugged gently at Tammy's leash. "I'm going home."

The uphill walk home was silent and tense. She was surprised to find an unfamiliar car parked in their driveway and a brunette stranger at their gate. When they came closer, the woman turned. "Ally, hi," she said, smiling widely. She couldn't be any older than twenty-five. "Talk about good timing!"

"This is Gabby," Ally explained. "We did a job at her dad's place yesterday."

Bron smiled politely. "Hello."

"How are your eyes?" Gabby asked Ally.

Ally grinned. "Perfect—now."

Gabby shifted on the spot. "You and Daniel were gone before I was back from town." She reached out, handing an envelope to Ally. "Here's the rest of what Dad owes you."

"You didn't have to rush it over," Ally said.

Gabby shook her head. "Oh, it's no trouble."

Bron took in the way Gabby's gaze tracked Ally. It was obvious. Gabby was infatuated. "Maybe I'll bump into you in town?" Gabby said, backing away toward her car.

Ally nodded. "I'm sure. Thanks again, Gabby."

Opening the gate, Bron smiled good-bye to Gabby and tugged on Tammy's leash. As she started up the driveway, she heard Gabby's car reversing. Seconds later Ally was beside her.

"So are you fucking her too?"

Ally scoffed. "Not biting, Bron. I'm done arguing with you."

Bron stopped to undo the metal clip of Tammy's leash and the dog sprinted up the hill in search of her water bucket. "Do I need to get tested?" she asked bluntly.

Up ahead, Ally spun. Her eyes widened. "What?"

"Have you been tested recently?"

"I was tested a year ago," Ally said simply.

Bron's eyes widened, her blood boiling. "A *year* ago? Are you fucking kidding me?"

Ally clicked her tongue. "I hadn't been with anybody for two years before last night."

Bron paused, the weight of the confession catching her off-guard. Was that why Ally had been so responsive to her touch? *Two years?* "I don't believe you," Bron said.

Ally's stare penetrated Bron's. She shrugged and walked away from the conversation toward the house. "Believe what you want, Bron. But do you really think I'm so selfish that I'd put you at risk if I didn't know for sure that I was clean?"

Just as Bron was beginning to prepare dinner, Jackie called from the McDonald's alongside the highway, the halfway point between Sydney and the mountains. Although her stepmother had always been a great long distance driver, she could hear the tiredness in her voice. "I was so glad to get Daniel's call this morning, I tell you. *Thank God* the fires have been contained. Bloody Carol was starting to drive me up the wall."

"Was she?" Bron asked distractedly, peering out the kitchen window. Daniel had returned and was out on the veranda with Ally, going over the job list for the next week.

"She wanted to come everywhere with us," Jackie continued. "And I didn't mind at first, but then we got to the zoo, and she wanted to have a whinge about the price of the bloody ticket, the food, everything."

She chuckled. "That's Carol."

"I couldn't stand another night there, Bron. She's my sister and I love her to death but she's a loon."

With Annie and Jackie eating at the highway rest stop, Bron began slicing enough broccoli, carrots and potato to go with the chicken for herself, Ally and Daniel. On the top of the fridge, the radio had been tuned to the local channel. For once, Bron didn't detest the overplayed Christmas tunes. While they usually did her head in each Christmas, she could only think of Annie and how excited she would be on Christmas morning when she realized that yes, there was Santa Claus.

She watched through the window as Ally disappeared around the veranda. Moments later, her feet padded down the hall, and as she came into the kitchen, she could feel Ally's dark stare on her back.

She pressed a gentle hand to the small of Bron's back and a tremor of excitement travelled up her spine, the hairs at the base of her neck standing of their own accord.

"I'm sorry," Bron said softly.

Ally nodded. "So am I."

Annie was over the moon to be home, and Bron was over the moon to be reunited with her niece. Annie chatted nonstop about her Sydney adventures, and when she finally drew breath, Bron asked, "So it wasn't all that bad, was it?"

After they'd unpacked the car, bringing load after load of photo albums, bags and storage containers back into the house,

Jackie was adamant about getting the washing done that night. She'd been in the laundry for no longer than a minute when she wandered into the kitchen.

Left to clean the kitchen alone, Bron glanced at her. "What's up?" she asked.

"Ally's sheets were still in the dryer."

In the sink, Bron's hands tightened on the lip of a dinner plate. Heat rose to her cheeks. She placed the sudsy plate on the drying rack with extra caution. "Are they?"

"Mmm," Jackie hummed. "I should give them to her. Wouldn't want her sleeping on a bare mattress *again*."

With her back to Jackie, Bron rolled her eyes at a handful of dirty cutlery, knowing that her mother knew very well that Ally had not slept in her own bed. She dropped the knives and forks into the sink and reached for the tea towel to dry her hands. "I'll do it." Avoiding her mother's gaze, she took the sheets from Jackie's arms.

Silently cursing the armful of bedsheets, Bron took the stairs two at a time. By the time she reached the top landing, the shower had shut off. In an effort to not make a sound, Bron manipulated the bathroom doorknob and stepped inside.

Standing before her, completely naked, Ally grinned. "Hey—"

She gestured wildly with the sheets in her arms. "You left your sheets in the dryer!"

"Oh, thanks," Ally said obliviously. "Can you pop them on my bed?"

"No," Bron hissed. "Mum knows!"

Ally blinked twice. "What?"

"Mum knows you didn't sleep in your bed!"

When realization dawned on her, Ally laughed. She moved closer, her nude form dampening the sheets. She grasped Bron's face in her warm, wet hands, and pressed their lips together.

It took a moment for Bron's lips to catch up, and even when they did, she still couldn't relax. She was hyperaware of Ally's stiff nipple pressing against the back of her hand that curled around the sheets. Ally quickly sensed her rigid state, and without breaking the kiss, took the sheets from her arms and dropped them onto the lid of the toilet. This time, her needy hands found home on Bron's hips, her fingers flexing as she pulled Bron closer. Bron's hands suddenly had a will of their own, reaching out to grasp the slim curve of Ally's waist, pressing them together.

Ally's mouth ran across the junction of her neck and shoulder, and Bron gasped softly. "I have to put Annie to bed."

Ally didn't pull away. "You feel so good." Her lips parted and her tongue skimmed across Bron's freckled skin. Bron's eyes closed. She seemed to liquefy at the touch. Had anyone ever wanted her this much?

"Bron," Ally murmured, her mouth closing over Bron's collarbone.

With a hand on Ally's jawline, Bron brought the taller woman's lips back to hers. For a moment longer, she indulged them both before she slowly withdrew.

Ally's eyes were starving. "Can I come to you tonight?"

Annie's footsteps at the bottom of the stairs were loud and forewarned the immediate call of her name. She quickly let herself out of the bathroom and closed the door behind her. She took a few large steps down the hall just as Annie rounded the top of the staircase.

Annie twisted on the spot. "Nanna says bedtime. Eugh."

"Yep, bedtime. You've had a very big day."

"Can I please sleep with you tonight?" Annie asked softly.

Annie had been all over Bron since she'd gotten home, crawling up into her lap, peppering her with kisses. She'd stalled during bath time as she revelled in Bron's undivided attention. Bron had sat on the toilet lid, watching tiredly as the shampoo bottle and Safari Barbie fought over—of all things—the last table at a busy restaurant. Of course, the soap holder was the restaurant table. What on earth had she been watching at Carol's?

"Please?" Annie whined.

She was torn between her motherly instinct and Ally's request. She knew when it came to Annie, she'd have to put her foot down eventually. As sweet as her sister was, Libby had never indulged Annie enough to let the little girl have such a strong hold over her.

"No," Bron said firmly. "There's no reason why you can't sleep in your own bed tonight."

"But, Aunty Bron…" Annie moaned.

"Al's in the bathroom," Bron changed the subject. "Go and knock and wish her a good night. Then bed."

As the finale of a cooking competition drew to an end on TV, Bron and Ally exchanged glances across the lounge room. Next to her, Jackie turned her head. Bron quickly focused back on the TV. She shifted on the lounge, pressing her thighs together in an effort to relieve as much of the building pressure as she could until she wished her family good night.

Brushing her teeth, Bron heard Ally's feet on the stairs. The toothbrush stalled at the back of her mouth, and she stared into the mirror for a moment until she heard the sound of Libby's bedroom door closing. When she stepped back into the hall, the house was in darkness. Everybody had gone to sleep.

Bron laid awake, listening to the pitter-patter of raindrops as they sprinkled against the tarp covering the tray of Daniel's ute. She had barely been in bed fifteen minutes when her bedroom door opened and closed behind Ally, followed by the soft click of the lock. Without a word, Ally slipped into her bed and pressed against Bron. Her breath fanned Bron's lips. "Is this okay?" Ally whispered.

"Yes."

Her palm tracked Ally's abdomen across the thin cotton of her ribbed singlet to her back. Their bare legs tangled as Bron peeled off her own singlet and then Ally's, tossing them both to the end of the mattress.

Ally was smiling into their kiss. She could feel it. Ally pulled back, her lips travelling lower, over Bron's jawline, to the base of her throat and her sternum. Those lips found one of Bron's nipples, and her body arched into the touch, her mind completely blank. When Ally abandoned the nipple she had lovingly suckled, in order to pay homage to the other, the cool breeze stiffened the tip even more so.

Bron glanced down, wanting—needing—to see what it looked like to have Ally's lips against her chest again. There was little light in the room, but she could make out the perfect line of Ally's nose, the darkness of her brows. *Oh, god.*

She closed her eyes and relaxed against the pillows as Ally's ravenous mouth moved south. Nothing had ever, would ever, feel this good, Bron thought. She wet her lips as a ferocious and untamed anticipation fired in her chest. But that feeling was immediately followed by an awareness that was much larger, almost too devastating to accept when Ally's warm lips were already *there*, working against her so softly, so gently.

I'm in love with her.

CHAPTER FOURTEEN

Bron was on the veranda lapping up the end of a full, uninterrupted afternoon of work when Annie came skipping up the hill of the driveway, sans her oversized backpack. Bron laid her pencil down on the sketch and sighed that her few hours of solitude had drawn to a close.

Granted an early leave by Daniel, Ally had said she'd pick up Annie to give Bron some extra sketching time.

When she thanked her over the phone, Ally had joked, "I'm expecting something out of it, you know."

With Jackie in the room, she'd fumbled for a reply, finally settling on, "I don't doubt it."

She didn't. It had been almost two weeks since the fire and since they'd first slept together. And it seemed as though Ally was still very much into her. Only a few nights had gone by that they hadn't slept together. When Annie hadn't monopolized the empty space in her bed, Ally was there, slipping in next to Bron after the house had fallen silent and withdrawing from the warmth of Bron's body just before the sun rose.

She squinted in the bright sun, wondering how far behind her niece Ally fell.

"How was your last day of school for the year, missy?" Bron called.

"It was good," Annie said as she rounded the driveway. "Hardly anybody went to school, so we had a pizza party and watched movies all day."

Tammy bounded across the front yard at full speed, appearing as though she would almost bowl Annie over, but she skidded to a stop directly in front of her, anticipating the moment Annie's skinny little arms would envelop her. "Ally's got a surprise for you..." Annie sing-songed.

Bron pulled the cover over her sketchpad, watching as Tammy licked a cringing, laughing Annie all over her face and neck. "A surprise for me?"

Annie reefed open the front screen door, already reaching behind her neck for the zipper of her dress. "Can't tell, won't tell!"

For a brief second, Bron was stumped. A surprise? Ally hadn't gone out and done anything stupid like buy a car, had she? Had she found a different job? *Oh god, please don't let it be a stray animal.*

As soon as she saw Ally with a handful of mail, it clicked. Bron grinned, pride swelling in her chest. "You got the mail," she observed.

It was easy to guess by Ally's ear-splitting grin and the way she looked down at an opened white envelope in her hands for a brief, reverent moment that she was attempting to rein in her excitement. She dropped Annie's backpack on the bottom step and leaned against the post of the veranda, smiling up at Bron.

"Congratulations, Al," Bron said warmly. "Getting into uni is a huge deal."

Ally shrugged modestly, but her pride was too pure, too good to be masked. "I start in February. I'll only have to go in once a week for a seminar, but the rest is completely online. I mean it comes out of my student loan, so it's not totally free, but you know..." She trailed off, the corners of her lips curling into a brilliant grin. "Plus, I get a free laptop."

Bron's first instinct was to offer to buy one for Ally, but she stopped herself. As much as she wanted to help make things easier for her, she knew Ally was fiercely independent. It was so profoundly important to her that she was building a life for herself. Bron deeply respected that. She walked down the porch steps and stopped at the last so that she was at eye level with Ally.

"You think I'm pretty hotshot now?" Ally asked cockily.

She clicked her tongue, amusement tugging at the corners of her mouth. Ally's eyes glistened as she watched Bron closely, trying to read her. A weight in Bron's abdomen pulled pleasantly. She had never seen such sincere adoration reflected in another woman's gaze.

Bron licked her lips. "Yeah. I think you're pretty hotshot."

"I can start paying you board real soon. Dan, can you pass the butter? And then with my *fancy* new diploma I can get my own place and get out of your hair for—"

At Ally's abrupt stop, Bron looked up from her steak. She followed the direction of Ally's stunned gaze to where Annie sat beside her. Annie was holding a half cob of corn by the cob holders, staring down at it in disbelief. The sun-coloured pillow of kernels was tainted blood red.

"Oh no," Annie said shakily, her lips parting and revealing the front gap where, until then, an only slightly wobbly tooth had resided. Her very first loose tooth now hung from a thread over her bottom lip. Dainty fingers reached up to touch the overhanging tooth. Annie's eyes widened. The kitchen fell completely silent. Each adult watched Annie with rapt attention, waiting on baited breath for Annie's outburst at the sight of blood on her fingertips. Thankfully, Ally dropped her fork to clap enthusiastically. "This is so exciting, Ann!"

For a brief moment, Annie weighed the possibility of excitement entering the equation. Quickly, her face brightened. "The tooth fairy is going to come tonight!" she informed the table.

The five of them went up to the bathroom. The four adults looked between themselves, silently arguing who it would be to do the honours. Jackie, Bron and Daniel looked to Ally. The brunette sighed in defeat.

"I can't watch," Jackie mumbled dramatically and disappeared.

Bron stood beside her brother, watching as Ally knelt down on the bathmat in front of Annie. She inspected the hanging tooth for a moment before finding a tissue to soak up the little bit of blood. Bron felt her own eyebrows rise as she watched Ally grip the hanging tooth. "Just be careful, Al," she inserted without censoring herself.

Fear cast over Annie's face at Bron's slip. Annie looked into Bron's eyes and then Ally's.

"Bron," Ally chastised, her focus entirely on Annie. "It's all good. Everything's good," Ally told Annie. She must have been smiling that smile she reserved just for Annie because the little girl's shoulders rose and fell with a deep breath, and her expression relaxed.

"Okay, Annie," Ally said. "Tell me how you want to do this. Do you want to count to three, or five, or ten?"

Before Annie could decide on the length of her countdown, Ally had covered the loose tooth with the tissue and quickly pulled it. Daniel laughed and Bron shot a scolding glance in his direction.

"Look," Ally said, holding the tooth in the bloody tissue.

In shock, Annie started to tear up. "You tricked me," she whispered, poking her tongue through the vacant space in her bottom row of teeth. As entitled as she was to loathe Ally in that moment, instead she fell into Ally's arms, allowing a chuckling Ally to pepper her cheeks with kisses.

"But wasn't it better that I tricked you? Look how wonderful you were! So brave!" As Ally lifted a hand to hold the back of a teary Annie's head, something inside Bron swelled at seeing Ally so nurturing. When Annie pulled back, Ally held the tooth up to Annie's eye level. "Where's this going to go, baby?"

In the space of twenty-four hours, Bron found herself playing the roles of Tooth Fairy, Aunt, Sister, Daughter, Lover, and Santa Claus. On a rainy Saturday afternoon, the day after Toothgate, Bron and Ally made the half-hour drive out to the big shopping complex a few suburbs over to finish their Christmas shopping.

As she circled the first level of the car park, she realised that everybody in a forty-kilometer radius had decided on the same thing. It was the twenty-third of December, and the final thirty-six hours of Christmas shopping had begun, so why had she expected anything less? She pulled into the long queue up to the second level and turned down the crackling radio. "Why don't we get Annie something from the both of us?" she suggested.

Worry had settled upon Bron not forty-eight hours before. Ally would be scraping the bottom of the barrel to buy something nice for Annie, as well as presents for the rest of them. Bron didn't want that.

Ally's expression was blank for a moment before it clouded over with pride. "We can go halves," she said firmly. "If we pool our money, we could get her a bigger Santa present too."

Bron frowned. That wasn't what she had meant.

Ally sighed. "I know what you're doing. Unless you're planning on getting her one of those iPad things as well, I can afford a kid's bike."

"Why do you have to be so proud?" Bron asked, relieved that the queue was finally moving.

"I'm aware you're Little Miss Moneybags, but I can manage to pay for half of Annie's bike. Or at least a wheel," Ally joked.

Bron laughed. "I'm not rich. I'm…comfortable."

Ally reached across the console and rested a hand just above Bron's knee. "So am I."

Ten minutes later, after tailing a mother with a pram with the stalking skill of a paparazzo, Bron had found parking. Ally's hand found hers as they crossed the parking lot.

"Al?" Bron asked when they reached the sliding glass doors of the entrance.

"Yeah?"

"I don't need anything, okay?"

Ally smirked, squeezing Bron's fingers before letting them go. "I'll meet you outside Toys R Us at half-past three?"

Bron remained curious about Ally's destinations. They didn't cross paths in the CD store or jeweller where Bron purchased two of Jackie's presents, or in the home entertainment section of Target where Bron picked up the portable speakers for Daniel. As she made her way around the centre, Bron encouraged herself not to search for Ally. She made such an effort not to spy, that she couldn't really blame herself when, halfway up the escalator to Level Three, she looked down to see Ally outside Regan's Jewellers, the same store Bron had visited not half an hour before. Ally was stuffing a tiny, dark blue plastic bag—a Regan's bag—into a larger paper bag. Had Ally bought her jewellery? She quickly averted her gaze, but the damage had been done. She'd already seen too much.

Choosing a gift for Ally proved harder than she'd anticipated. She wanted to get Ally something meaningful, but at the same time, she didn't want to risk upstaging her. What if Ally hadn't been in the jeweller buying her a gift? What if she'd only bought Jackie a plain necklace, and on Christmas morning, Bron opened Ally's gift to find a book or a DVD? If she went too crazy, like she had on the camera for Ally's birthday, her pride would be irrevocably damaged.

The money matter was a sore point. The reality was that, with the royalties from her books, she'd been more than comfortable for a long time. Her sunny, spacious one-bedroom Back Bay apartment may not have been Beacon Hill, but it was still relatively upmarket. The only reason she'd ever had overdue electricity or water bills was simply because she forgot to pay them, not because she couldn't. Even during the year-long period she'd sent large cheques home to help Libby when Annie was little, Bron had barely missed the extra money. In the last four months, she'd come to realize that, although they weren't strapped for cash, the rest of her family, and Ally, lived quite differently.

Inside the bookshop, she headed straight to the children's section. If there was one thing she could fault Libby on, it was not providing enough books for Annie. She was going to fix that. She scanned the shelves for a title that would interest Annie, her gaze catching every so often on the spine of a picture book or chapter book she'd illustrated. She selected a few chapter books for young readers, hoping they weren't too difficult for Annie. She was an intelligent six-year-old, but at the first sign of struggle, her interest always waned. Bron smiled, wondering just how well a gift of books was going to go down with her. Unenthusiastically, she assumed. *Maybe Santa can play bad cop with the books*, Bron thought.

On her way to the counter, she wandered past the gift table and stopped. Between an arrangement of Louisa May Alcott's *Little Women* and a few Austen titles sat a gorgeous brown satchel bag that immediately caught her eye. When she picked it up, she found that it was a soft leather. The image of it hanging off Ally's shoulder as she left for university was vivid. The fact that it wasn't a designer label made it all the more perfect.

After making her purchase, she went straight back to the car park and hid the satchel bag beneath her seat. She contemplated leaving the presents she'd bought for Annie, Daniel and Jackie in the car too, but knowing that Ally would quickly figure her out, she carried those back into the centre with her.

When she rounded the corner to Toys R Us, Ally was standing patiently at the front of the store.

"Sorry to keep you waiting," she said. "I just checked my phone and realized I let time get away from me."

Ally raised her eyebrows. "That's okay." She grinned. "You're out of breath. I don't know, Bron. You might have to bring those half-hour morning runs of yours up to the full hour. You've got a good seven years on me and you're going to need to be able to keep up."

She rolled her eyes at the joke and let Ally take her hand again. As they made their way toward the sports section at the back, a young mother did a double take at their clasped hands and quickly averted her gaze. She groaned inwardly. After living in Boston for so long, she'd forgotten there were still homophobic pockets of society.

Apparently, she wasn't the only one who caught the snide glance. "I think we're scaring the children," Ally joked, her grip on Bron's hand unwavering.

"God forbid."

In the sports section, Ally was like a big kid, immediately lifting a display bike as far as the security chain would allow it to be pulled from its stand. "This one is cool."

She inspected the back of it. "She's going to need training wheels. Will they be able to go over that hubcap?"

Ally scoffed. "Nope, no training wheels. Forget it. Out of the question."

"Good luck with that, Al. She's the most uncoordinated child I've ever seen. I don't need a broken arm."

"You won't have one. Annie will."

"Yeah, and I don't need to drive her forty minutes to the nearest hospital."

"You won't have to. She's not going to break anything. I'll teach her to ride it."

Bron sat down on a bike seat. "How much is it?"

Ally lifted the tag that was hanging over the handlebars. "One ninety."

She inspected the bright green glittery paint. "She's going to scratch it."

"Oh?" Ally feigned surprise. "Well, if I'd known that, I would have suggested we just pick her up one from the local tip."

Bron chuckled. If somebody had told her six months ago that the most important thing that Christmas would be deciding on the right bike for a six-year-old—*with Ally Shepherd*—she would have called them foolish.

Ally swung a leg over the bike and sat on the low seat. She pedalled as far as the chain would allow and pulled on the brakes, the wheels screeching across the white linoleum floor. Bron's eyebrows shot up. "Ally," she hissed. "You'll get in trouble."

"You're cute when you're being a Goody Two-shoes."

"I'm not a Goody Two-shoes. I stole something once."

Ally scoffed. "What did you steal? A packet of sugar from a food court?"

"I was fourteen and I stole a pair of headphones from the old Grace Brothers store in the city."

"You sound proud."

Bron frowned. "Mum had just died. I was acting out."

Ally nodded. She chewed at her lip, clearly thinking. "I've never stolen anything," she said after a moment.

"Really?" Bron said, attempting to shroud the surprise in her voice.

Ally thought for a moment. "Nope. Never."

Respect for Ally flared inside of her, fuelling deep attraction. She was quickly learning that Ally wore morality very well. She wondered if she was blushing. "I'm going to go and find someone to help us. Just don't get any more out."

"Yes, dear."

As Bron reached the end of the aisle, Ally flicked the bell on the bike, its ring echoing loudly. Bron turned around, her grip tightening on the handles of her handbag.

Ally grinned as Bron playfully shook her head and went to find a sales assistant.

Much to Ally's delight, they purchased the sparkly green bike with its bell and basket. Ally was adamant about the training wheels, refusing the sales assistant's offer to add on anything more than a matching green helmet. Sighing, Bron let Ally finalize the transaction, enjoying Ally's proud show of declining the muscular young boy's assistance to get the bike to the car, her forearms flexing as she skilfully manoeuvred the heavy box into a trolley and pushed it through the centre.

Once they had the box in the boot of the car and had covered it with an old picnic blanket in case Annie ran out to greet them when they arrived home, Ally turned to Bron. "Can I buy you a coffee? Or a Frappuccino? Or whatever hot milky beverage you Yanks drink?" She wrapped her arms around Bron's waist to pull her closer, and leaned against the car. "I don't want to go home yet. I want you to myself for a little while longer."

Bron felt heat rise to her cheeks. "You may."

They found a table inside an air-conditioned café. "Do you mind if I'm rude for a moment and send an email?" Bron asked.

"I haven't been able to get a decent Wi-Fi signal at home since the fires."

"Sure." Ally leaned across the table. "What would you like?" she flirted.

Bron grinned, fully aware that Ally was waiting to hear her own name. "A latte," Bron coyly requested. She wiggled her eyebrows for extra effect.

Ally smiled widely. "'Kay." Her lips parted as though she were about to say more, but she stopped herself. "Be right back."

Bron watched Ally join the short queue at the counter. She was so unbelievably gorgeous, but Bron had known that for years. But, undeniably, the most stunning thing about Ally was her goodness. Just as she pondered the thought, Ally politely gestured to the elderly lady behind her to order in her place. How had she spent so long oblivious to what Libby saw in Ally? She'd been so suspicious of Ally when she'd first arrived home. And now? God, how wrong she had been.

She opened the drafts folder in her email account and located the one she'd debated sending for the last week. She scanned it over once more.

Alice,

I'm currently finishing up a project with Yellowstone Books, but I'd like to draw for your press when this project is complete—if you'll have me. At this point in time, I plan to relocate to Australia to be with my niece. As you are aware, my current contract with Yellowstone allows me to work on other books between projects, but when I formally relocate, I presume they will lessen my workload due to communication barriers. I plan on informing them of my plans next week. If you wish to set me up with an author, I'm happy to start in the New Year. I hope that, as you proposed, this can become a regular partnership.

Best,

Bronwyn

Her thumb hovered over the send icon. Once the email was sent, her decision was final. She would be coming home for good. So long, Boston. So long, MIT.

An exchange between Ally and the elderly lady at the counter caught her eye. She strained to hear what was being said, watching as Ally pointed to the 'NO EFTPOS' sign and said something to the lady. When Ally handed over a purple five-dollar note and generously told the old lady to take it, Bron figured the lady hadn't had enough cash on her, and Ally had stepped up to help.

Bron's chest tightened as Ally ordered and took their table number. As she headed back to Bron, the elderly lady reached out from her lonely table and tapped Ally's tattooed bicep, thanking her profusely. Bron didn't believe in signs from beyond the grave, but if Libby was going to send one, watching Ally's continuing exchange with the elderly woman seemed to be *enough*.

Bron tapped send and watched the email to Alice disappear. It was clear Ally was waiting for more than just coffee dates and casual sex, and Bron wanted to make sure she got what she ordered.

CHAPTER FIFTEEN

"So tell me again what you'd like Santa to bring you?" Ally asked Annie, who was skipping ahead of them down the footpath in the darkness.

Swiping at the thin film of sweat on her upper lip, Bron groaned. "Why would you ask her that at nine p.m. on Christmas Eve?" she mumbled lowly.

"Anything?" Annie wondered.

"Anything at all," Ally said, winking at Bron's scowl.

Bron braced herself for more unexpected additions or deletions to Annie's wish list. Annie was constantly changing her mind. Would it be a scooter instead of a bike? A new paddle pool instead of the Slip-N-Slide Bron had picked up at the twenty-four hour Kmart the night before? She worried she was spoiling Annie—that they all were—but this was Annie's first Christmas without her mother. It wasn't perfect parenting, she knew this, but if she could fill part of that enormous, missing gap with consumerism, that was exactly what she was going to do.

Thankfully, Annie's request was one that Bron could fulfil. "I would wish for Aunt Bron never to go back to America and live here with us forever."

As Annie skipped ahead, Bron and Ally fell into an uncomfortable silence. Her mind reeled with conflicting emotions—the utter joy of being so needed, so *wanted*, by Annie, and anxiety over Ally's frustration. She wanted nothing more than to confide in Ally, to tell her that she wasn't going anywhere, but something had been holding her back in the twenty-four hours—no, thirty hours—since she'd sent the email and received Alice's ecstatic reply. While she knew Ally deserved to know, she didn't know if telling Ally privately, separately from the rest of the family, was the best way to go about it. Would it put too much pressure on their relationship? Was she being too presumptuous? The last thing she wanted was for Ally to think she'd suddenly made the decision solely because she wanted a future for the two of them—even if there was some truth to it. While Annie's wellbeing was a major part of the decision, she knew she would be lying to herself if she said it wasn't because she wanted Ally in her life too. Ally had made it clear she wanted Bron and Annie to stay in Australia, but what if that changed once Ally had her own place? Once they put some distance between them, would Ally have less of an investment in Bron? In Annie? The last thought made her nauseous.

"Annie," Bron called out. "Stop outside the gate, please."

When Bron and Ally caught up to Annie at the bottom of the hill, they found themselves amongst a large crowd gathered on the nature strip who obviously shared their idea of how to spend the last few hours of Christmas Eve. The Queenslander home at the end of the street had an amazing setup. The previous year, the house had been featured in the Sydney Morning Herald Christmas lift-out as one of top twenty decorated homes in Greater Sydney.

Annie looked up at Bron in awe of the brightly decorated house, as though they hadn't driven past the house a number of times at night in the past thirty days and seen it in all its illuminated glory. Jackie had even walked Annie down there earlier in the week to see the snow machine and food truck the home owners had hired to impress the visiting Channel Nine news team.

"Can we please go inside?" Annie begged, her blond hair bathed extra golden in the white lights. "You will both love it. I promise!"

Bron dropped a gold coin in the donation bucket as they went in, gladdened to read the sticker on the side of the bucket and know that the proceeds were going to the Rural Fire Service. In the opened garage of the house, Santa Claus sat on a plastic garden chair in a pair of tropical-printed board shorts and his classic red jacket. Bron wondered if she'd ever seen anything so Australian.

The three of them joined the small queue of young children and their parents for a photo and chat with Surfer Santa. When they were next in line, Ally asked Annie, "Are you ready to tell Santa what you want?" Nervously licking her lips, Annie nodded. "Don't forget your pleases and thank yous."

"Ah, Miss Annie," Santa said. "So happy to see you back again!"

Annie grinned widely at the sound of her name. Bron was impressed by Surfer Santa's memory, but then again, Annie was a gorgeous child—inside and out. She wasn't easy to forget.

As Annie climbed up onto Santa's lap, he began a deep and meaningful conversation about the woes of sleigh travel, Ally turned her camera on and moved across the room to get a better shot. Although Bron and Jackie had already taken Annie to have her annual Santa photo at the shopping centre weeks ago, Ally had insisted on bringing along her camera to take a few shots. The professional photos of Annie in her good dress, her hair perfectly brushed and angelic were perfect. But even before Bron saw Ally's shots—Annie in her overalls, her hair in two braids, front tooth missing, sitting on Surfer Santa's lap in a neighbour's garage down the street—Bron knew they would be far more precious.

Santa motioned to Ally. "Is this your aunt you want to stick around a bit longer?"

Ally lowered the camera and forced a smile. She motioned with a thumb to Bron. "That'd be the other one, Santa."

"Well, Annie," he said, "I've been watching you on my North Pole camera, and I can see you're very lucky to have an aunt like yours."

Bron could feel her eyes watering at the compliment. Although she'd never met the man, she imagined he knew about Libby's accident—the whole town did. He was obviously putting a face to the name of the aunt who had returned home to parent her niece.

In her peripheral vision, Bron could feel Ally watching her. When Bron looked across the room, teary-eyed, Ally only allowed their gazes to meet for a moment before she left the garage and headed over to the window displays. With a glance back at Annie, who was deep in conversation with Santa, Bron followed her.

She crossed the front lawn and stood next to Ally. Silently, they admired the intricate display behind glass, the faint notes of *The Little Drummer Boy* raining down from a speaker set up somewhere above them on the roof. The snow-clad town inside reminded her of Boston. An intricately decorated carousel revolved in the centre of the display next to the town Christmas tree. It was so like the one that would be standing in Boston Common until the beginning of January, an annual gift from Nova Scotia for their assistance during the Halifax Explosion a century before. At the back of the display, Santa was making his way down a red-bricked chimney. Fireplaces were lit inside the miniature houses, and in the foreground, carollers sang to the townsfolk. She sighed at the simplicity of the miniature world in front of her.

"I've always loved displays like this, but imagine getting all of this out every December, and then having to pack it all away. I mean, it's worth it, but I don't envy—"

"I'm in love with you, Bron," Ally said, her voice so low and broken that Bron instantly felt faint. "I've loved you for a really long time. And I know I'm a pretty complicated person. I'm trying really fucking hard to adjust to being out of Oberon, and I know it might look like I have my shit together, but...I don't.

Not yet." The pleasant ache low in Bron's belly ignited once again as Ally searched Bron's features for a reaction. The soft white glow from the display threw shadows across the sharp lines of Ally's face, her square jaw, her perfect nose. *She's so beautiful.* "I'm too reckless," Ally asserted, her voice hoarse. "But as much as I know that I'm no good for you, I know other things which kind of make up for it, I think, maybe…" She shoved her hands deep in the pockets of her denim shorts. "I know that you're still in a lot of pain," she said softly, "pain over losing Libby, about what's best for Annie. But I think I can make you feel better." Her voice dropped an octave when she continued, "I don't want to say I can fix you, because you're not broken, but I've never wanted anyone the way I want you. The way I want to be with you. You make me feel like a *good person*, and I want to be good." Bron watched her visibly swallow. "I just think you're so…" she trailed off. "I just need you to know that I love you."

Bron licked her lips. *Tell her.*

Ally cleared her throat. "You don't have to say it back," she whispered.

Before she could find words, Annie was running across the grass and coming toward them. "He looked different than the other Santa at the shops," she said mindlessly. "But I like him better because he always knows my name. He says I have to go to bed very soon because this street is his next stop, and we don't live very far up."

Bron looked up at Ally who was focused on the carousel in the display, her jawline tensed, her eyes shining with unshed tears. *Oh, Ally.* Bron's heart pounded at the sight of her turmoil.

"Come on!" Annie whined, pulling on Bron's wrist.

"Can we finish this at home?" she whispered to Ally.

Ally nodded. "I just need a minute," she said, her voice coarse. "But I'll be right behind you."

After Bron spent the better half of an hour setting out milk and biscuits for Santa, and under Annie's instruction some carrots for the reindeers, she was finally able to get an animated Annie into bed. "Now don't you come downstairs to the lounge room to sneak a peek, because Santa knows when you're sleeping, and he definitely knows when you're awake!" She sing-songed, pulling the top sheet over Annie's shoulders. *Also, I have to spend the next two hours assembling your bicycle, and I'd prefer to do so in the coolest room in the house, which just so happens to be the lounge room.*

Downstairs, Bron found Ally at the kitchen sink slicing potatoes for the potato salad for Christmas lunch. Even over the gentle stream running from the tap, there was no way Ally wouldn't have heard her coming down the stairs and into the kitchen, but still, she didn't turn around.

Bron jiggled her car keys against her thigh. "I have to go pick up Mum from the church. I want to finish our conversation, believe me I do, but I'm already late. I'll be ten minutes—tops."

When Ally turned, her stare was blank. "Okay."

We'll talk when I get back, her pointed stare promised. Ally looked away.

She drove the few streets over and found Jackie waiting on the steps outside the church.

"Hey, Mum. Enjoy the free aircon?"

"Cheeky," Jackie admonished as she buckled her seat belt. "Enjoy the lights?"

She nodded.

"You're quiet," Jackie said when they stopped at the intersection of Main Street.

"Am I?"

"You are. Does it have anything to do with Miss Ally?"

"Why would it have anything to do with Ally?"

"You tell me."

"Can we not do this right now?" she pleaded. "It can be your Christmas present to me."

"Good, because I haven't had a chance to get you anything yet," Jackie kidded.

She chuckled. "Perfect."

By the time she arrived home with Jackie, Daniel was back from Carly's. She followed Jackie into the kitchen where Ally was still chopping potatoes. "Ah, not directly onto my sink!" Jackie scolded Ally. "Get a bloody chopping board out."

"Sorry, Jacks," Ally said, but none of the usual playfulness could be found in her tone.

"Make us a cuppa, will you, love?" Jackie asked Bron. "I've still got a few pressies to wrap upstairs."

"Can you tell Daniel to turn the telly down?" Bron called out to Jackie. "I don't need Annie making curtain calls."

She flicked open the lid of the kettle and filled it under the filter tap. Ally moved closer to place a dirtied pot in the sink. The liquid detergent foamed as Ally filled the sink to wash the pot. Just being closer to Ally drew a wave of peace over Bron. This *thing* between them was only growing stronger. She looked up at Ally. "You're not going to bed yet, are you?"

When Ally looked down at her, the intensity of her gaze bared her adoration, pure and sincere. Bron's heart raced. "Not yet. I've still got to put the bloody bike together—"

"I'll help you. I'll take a shower, and hopefully by then everyone else will be asleep." She placed a hand at the small of Ally's back. Ally tensed beneath her light touch. "And we can talk."

Ally licked her lips and went back to scrubbing the pot. "Go have your shower."

Bron passed the lounge room on the way upstairs. "I'm just going to have a shower," she told Daniel. "I'll say goodnight now because you'll probably be asleep when I come down."

Bron watched Daniel shrug indifferently, his attention focused on the television. "Maybe."

Bron sighed. "Well, goodnight then."

Daniel drew his gaze away from the television and looked his sister up and down. "Good night, weirdo?"

She groaned internally. Would she ever get Ally alone? She turned back toward the lounge room. "Oh, Al and I have to put the bike together, and we could really do with an extra hand."

That got him up off the lounge. "Nope. Your present, your problem. I'm going to bed."

She grinned. *Too easy.*

She climbed the stairs, her mind racing as she tried to sort through what Ally needed from her. *What should I start with?*

You're right, Annie is ours now. Was that too much pressure right off the bat? *I'm staying.* Perhaps? *I love you.* At the last thought, her entire body instantly buzzed with anticipation.

A whisper came from the master bedroom. "Bron, is that you?"

Bron poked her head into Jackie's room. A few presents were wrapped on top of the bedspread, and her mother was fiddling with sticky tape.

"Gosh, it's nice having you home on Christmas Eve," Jackie said softly. "I was absolutely dreading this Christmas...but you're here. Ally's here."

She smiled. "I'm happy we're all here together."

"I think Libby's here too," Jackie murmured gently. "She'll always be with us."

Bron's heart seemed to lodge in her throat. As she watched her mother fold the edges of the gift wrapping, her heart and mind were at odds with how to reply. She didn't believe in the afterlife. Jackie knew that. But Jackie's words were undeniably true. Libby would always be around. In the god-awful floral shower curtain she had once gifted Jackie, the age-old dent in the front bumper Libby had made during her second driving lesson at sixteen. But mostly, Libby would always be around in every little thing Annie said, every gesture she made. Choked for words, she nodded softly. "I love you, Mum."

"I love you too, darl."

She took a quick shower. When she stepped out of the bathroom, Jackie's and Daniel's bedroom doors were both closed. *Perfect.* Towel drying her hair, she descended the stairs.

On the hardwood floor in front of the colourfully-lit Christmas tree, Ally sat amongst what looked like poorly organized piles of bike parts. Bron's father's old aluminium toolbox was open beside her, aglow from the light of the television. The few pages of instructions that she'd stubbornly cast aside fluttered across the lounge room floor each time the large fan oscillated in the corner of the room.

Bron swallowed. It seemed she was going to have to start. It was only fair. Ally had been brave enough to start everything else between them.

"I love you," Bron whispered.

Ally looked up.

Bron pressed her temple to the cool wood of the doorframe. "I should have said it earlier tonight. I'm sorry."

Ally gently dropped a spanner and sat back on her heels. "Come here," she whispered, her voice lower and huskier than Bron had ever heard.

She let out a nervous laugh, avoiding Ally's gaze as she moved across the room and sat down, pulling her legs beneath her.

Ally's gaze was trained on her, intense and vibrant. She tilted Bron's chin up, and kissed her chastely. After a moment, she pulled back. She picked up the spanner again, refocusing intently on the handlebars she'd assembled while Bron had showered. But there was a splitting grin across her face that Bron figured hadn't been instigated by attaching an orange reflector to handlebars.

Ally handed her the bike seat and a sparkly green rod. "How about you grease the end of the rod, blondie?"

Bron smiled, took the seat from Ally's hands and set to work.

After two reruns of *Friends* and a good hour spent listening to Dr. Oz rant about heart health, the bike was finally standing in all its glory.

Bron ran her fingers across the little hairs at the back of Ally's neck as she clipped the cane basket to the handlebars. She littered kisses over the prominent ridges of Ally's spine, and felt Ally's body tremble beneath her lips. "It's two in the morning. Come to bed."

Ally stood back, inspecting their handiwork. "What if Annie sits on it and it collapses?"

Tiredly, Bron shoved the instructions and plastic coverings back into the box. "Then she'll realize Santa's not very competent." She pushed the box between the lounge and the wall, making sure it was completely out of sight. "Just think how wonderful she'll think you are when you're the one who fixes Santa's mistakes."

She turned off the fairy lights on the tree, the room instantly falling darker with just the light of television infomercials. She held the enormous Santa sack open wide while Ally lowered the bike into it. When it was completely swallowed by red satin, Ally tied the white bow of the sack around the thin flagpole. After double-checking that everything was ready for the morning, Bron flicked off the television.

Exhausted, they reached the top of the stairs. When Bron reached for Ally's hand and tugged on it, one of Ally's eyebrows rose at Bron's daring suggestion. "Annie will come in as soon as the sun is up," she warned.

Bron shrugged, hooking two fingers into the belt loops of Ally's shorts to pull her closer. "I don't care." She kissed Ally firmly, *surely*, and inched her thumbs beneath the hem of Ally's singlet. "I don't care," she repeated into the kiss, desperate for Ally to return the kiss with equal vigour.

Bron felt the moment Ally truly understood the gravity of her words. Ally's body gave into the kiss with a burning ferocity, her hands sliding over Bron's behind, hoisting her up against her. She hooked her legs around Ally's waist and grasped at her shoulders, her core twitching hotly at Ally's possessive hold, her promising kiss. A deep yearning ached in her chest, and Bron doubted it would ever quell.

At first, Bron thought she'd been so wrapped up in their kiss that the walk to her own room at the end of the hall had transpired too quickly. But then she heard the creak of Libby's door. She reached a hand out and grasped the doorjamb, halting Ally's step. She broke the kiss, her lips sliding across Ally's hot cheek to her ear. Ally's chest heaved, her breathing unsteady. "Hey, hey," Bron murmured. Ally moved a hand from Bron's behind, raking it up into her hair as she sucked at the tendons in Bron's neck. Bron shuddered. "Not Libby's room."

Ally nodded against her and swiftly walked them to the end of the hall. "Libby would have thrown a hissy fit if she was around to see this," Ally mumbled, her quiet laughter vibrating against Bron.

Bron giggled, a quiet peace overcoming her. There were so many things Bron desperately wanted to tell her baby sister about as each day passed. One day, if she ever got to see Libby again, her unbridled love for Ally Shepherd would be at the top of the list.

CHAPTER SIXTEEN

It wasn't Annie who woke Bron on Christmas morning—but a loud bang. The wooden stick holding the window ajar cracked under the pressure. The noise of the window slamming down threw Bron upright in bed. Ally sat up against her, the light sweat on their bodies cooling in the morning breeze.

Bron's hand grasped Ally's forearm. "The window stick snapped," she whispered softly, surprised that the glass hadn't shattered.

Wiping a hand over her face, Ally tried to find her bearings in the semidarkness. "What's the time?" she slurred.

The sun had already begun its ascent over the hill. Bron looked to the digital clock on her bedside table. "Twenty to six."

For a prolonged moment, they listened for any sound indicating the noise had woken Annie. When the house remained silent, Ally pressed an effortless kiss to Bron's bare shoulder blade and slid back down the mattress.

Her body still humming from the sudden wake-up, Bron sat up against the headboard and ran a hand through her hair. She felt across the mattress for the singlet she always slept in, and eventually found it wedged halfway underneath Ally's pillow.

She sat quietly for a moment, looking down at Ally, naked in her bed. Her breath caught when she realized Ally was wide awake, her eyes open and watching Bron.

She smiled softly, reaching out to trail her fingers across Ally's hairline. Her heart was full. They basked in the serene moment until Ally shifted. She pressed a kiss to Bron's lips, pulled herself up to sit on the edge of the bed, and began to dress.

"You don't have to go back to your room. I thought I made that clear last night," she whispered.

After pulling her own singlet over her head, Ally rested a hand against the mattress and focused on Bron. "You did. I'm not going back to my room," she whispered. "I just need to get something."

"Oh." Bron hugged her knees to her chest. "Okay."

She waited patiently for Ally to return to the room. Her body vibrated with the little amount of sleep she'd had in the last few days, but it pulsed with a childish excitement too. Today was going to be a good day.

When Ally masterfully tiptoed around the heavy creaking door and back into the room, she kneeled on the mattress beside Bron. She nervously fumbled with a wrapped little box in her hand. The certainty that it was jewellery was as terrifying as it was tremendous.

"I didn't want to give this to you in front of everyone." Ally wouldn't meet her gaze, fixing it on the bedsheet instead. "I didn't want to embarrass you or anything."

"Ally…"

Ally placed the gift in her lap. She slowly unwrapped it, noting that Ally had gone out and bought her own wrapping paper, opting not to use the few rolls the entire family had used on everybody's presents. After casting the paper aside, Bron held a navy box with silver trim in her hands. Her heart hammered as she lifted the lid.

She'd been given pearls and sapphires by Rae, which were hidden at the back of a drawer in her apartment in Boston, but never had a piece of jewellery made her heart swell the way the simple silver bracelet in the box did.

"You can return it if you don't like it," Ally said as Bron carefully pried the delicate chain from the pillow box with her middle finger and thumb.

"Al," she sighed. "It's beautiful. I love it. Thank you." She gestured for Ally to clasp it to her wrist.

"When I bought it, the girl asked me who it was for," Ally whispered, her fingertips dancing across Bron's inner wrist. Bron grinned down at the bracelet as Ally locked the clasp. "I told her it was for my girlfriend."

She read the loyalty and fulfilment in Ally's vulnerable gaze. She couldn't help the way her eyes dropped to Ally's lips. She ran her thumb across Ally's chin and drew her lips to her own. She felt Ally smile into the kiss.

"I'm staying. I'm moving home."

A moment of silence passed between them. "Really?" Ally breathed.

Bron drifted her fingers across Ally's prominent collarbone. "Yes." She gently pressed a hand against Ally's sternum. "I've already notified my press, and I've got a new job lined up in Sydney."

Ally's eyes bored into her. "And the job?"

Bron swallowed. She shook her head and willed herself not to get teary at the thought that MIT no longer had a place in her future.

Ally's expression was tentative. "Are you sure?"

She nodded. "I have to pack up everything in Boston. It'll take a couple of weeks. I thought I could take Annie with me?" She phrased it as a question, respectful of Ally's opinion. "Maybe we can stopover in Los Angeles so she can have a few days at Disneyland. She goes back to school at the very end of January, so I want to have her back in time for her first day."

Ally smiled. "I think that's a really good idea." She paused. "So you'll be leaving soon?"

She nodded. "After New Year. But when I come home…it'll be for good. I think I want to look into getting my own place in town too. As much as Mum likes having us here for company, she's getting older and she needs her own space."

Ally kissed her firmly.

"I wish you could come with us to the States," Bron said. "Parole's a bitch."

Ally leaned back against the headboard, her face inches from Bron's. "I know. I'm going to miss your…supervision."

Bron laughed softly. She swiped the pad of her thumb across Ally's lips. Ally kissed it, her chestnut gaze darkening.

Her bedroom door creaked open. Annie poked her head into the room. Annie was the cutest, most angelic thing Bron had ever seen, with bedhead, eyes squinty with sleep, in her little nightie. Too distracted to even realise the oddity of her aunt and Ally being in bed together, she shouted, "There's a flag in my Santa sack!" She was visibly wired with excitement, her hands gesturing wildly.

"A flag in your Santa sack?" Ally feigned curiously. "Maybe Santa brought you a golf course?"

"No, no," Annie said, struggling to handle the exhilaration bubbling through her. "It's, it's coming out the top," she sputtered. "I think it's a bike!"

"Oh, my goodness!" Bron gasped. "You lucky girl!"

"Can you please, *please* hurry?" Annie begged.

"Can you please, *please* go and wake up Nanna and Uncle Dan before you touch any presents?" Bron mocked. "And wake Nanna gently."

Annie was out the door before the last part of the instruction could fully leave Bron's lips.

The two sat still for a moment, listening as Annie told her grandmother that she'd already woken Ally too, "because Aunt Bron and Ally were having a sleepover" in Bron's room.

Ally made a sweeping motion over the crown of her head to indicate Annie's obliviousness. Bron laughed and Ally cut it off with a chaste kiss. "Merry Christmas, Santa," Ally murmured.

Just as Ally swung her legs over the edge of the bed, Jackie stopped in the doorway. She leaned against the doorjamb. "Merry Christmas, loveys."

Feeling herself flushing under Jackie's perceptive stare, Bron averted her gaze, reaching for a hair tie on her bedside table. "Merry Christmas, Mum," she said, pulling her hair into a ponytail.

"I heard that we had a sleepover," Jackie teased.

Ally grinned. "We did," she declared, a hint of rebellious teenage girl in her tone.

Silence fell upon the three women, but Ally's lingering grin was louder than words.

Jackie tightened the sash on her robe, the corners of her mouth twitching in a poorly suppressed smile. "I'm going to put the kettle on before missy moo passes out with excitement."

When Jackie was out of earshot, Ally chuckled. "Come on, Aunty Bron." She reached across the bed and squeezed Bron's knee. "I want my Christmas presents."

Bron took her tea from the coffee table and sat down cross-legged next to the tree. When Annie held open the laundry door to let Tammy in, the dog was utterly confused by the early morning excitement. Her tail wagged eagerly as she followed her littlest boss around the lounge room, appraising Annie as she informed Tammy which Santa sack belonged to each member of the family.

To little surprise, the bike was the first to be unwrapped from its Santa sack. Annie squealed with delight, running her tiny hands over the glittery paint of the mud guard. "Santa is just the best!" Annie whispered in amazement. "Can I ride it now?"

Bron grinned at Ally. "How about you open the rest of your presents first?"

On opposite sides of the tree, Bron and Ally read the labels on the gifts and handed them across the room to Daniel and

Jackie. Bron marvelled at the basket of art supplies that would last her a year. "Mum," Bron berated. "This is too much."

"Hogwash," Jackie replied, turning to Ally who had just unwrapped Jackie's gift to her—a pair of UGG boots. "Do they fit?" Jackie asked Ally as she strode across the room in them.

"They're a bit tight, Jacs," Ally said.

"They're supposed to be. Come here and let me feel where your big toe is," she commanded, as though Ally were no older than Annie and couldn't determine whether or not the shoes fit.

After Jackie asserted the UGGS didn't need exchanging, Ally was so preoccupied showering Annie with attention each time she opened a present, oohing and ahhing over the toys, that when there were only a handful of presents still under the tree, Bron knew most of them had to be for Ally. At the very back of the tree, she eyed the icicle-patterned gift box that contained the leather satchel.

Bron's gaze skirted around the room. Jackie focused on cutting an intricately tightened bow from the present Annie had made for her. Daniel reclined back in the lounge, his head buried in the instruction manual for the portable Bluetooth speakers Bron had given him. She pulled the box from under the tree and pushed it in Ally's direction until the cardboard corner lightly pressed into Ally's thigh.

"For me?"

Bron nodded. Ally reached across the coffee table for the extra pair of scissors. She cut the glossy white ribbon and lifted the lid. As she held up the bag, the corners of her lips twitched.

"Do you like it?" Bron asked.

"Yeah," Ally said huskily, running her hand over the smooth leather. "It's really great." She pressed her nose against it and inhaled. "Thought it must be real leather," she conceded with a wink. "This is a lot."

"So is this," Bron said softly, her fingers trailing over the fine silver chain of Ally's bracelet.

Ally held her gaze for a long moment. When she muttered, "I'll thank you properly later," Bron felt heat rise to her neck.

The base of the tree was cleared but for a few biscuit tins wrapped for Father Jeff and the neighbours. Jackie heaved herself up from the floor. "Who wants breakfast?"

From the floor Bron looked around at the mess. World War III had erupted in their lounge room without any of them noticing. Opened toy boxes were cast across the floor between small mountains of shredded wrapping paper and sliced ribbons. The Santa sacks, empty and lifeless, were draped over the lounge, the base of the tree, the coffee table where their empty mugs sat forgotten, an inch of cold, leftover tea in each. Bron had never seen a clean-up so impressive.

Without being prompted, Annie rounded the room and pressed thank-you kisses to everybody's cheeks, hugging her uncle, her grandmother and Ally. When it came to Bron's turn, Annie plonked herself down between Bron's legs. "Thank you for all of my presents, Aunty Bron. I love them all."

Bron pressed a kiss to Annie's temple. "You're welcome, baby."

"Annie," Ally said. She lifted up a smaller Santa sack. "You still have a present from Santa."

Annie got up and hurriedly padded over to Ally. She peeked inside. "Oh," she said, her despairing tone obvious. "Silly Santa went and got me books."

* * *

Bron was passing the potato salad across the backyard dining table to Father Jeff when Annie squealed at the top of her lungs. Bron looked up and, for what seemed like the hundredth time that day, watched Annie slide to a stop at the end of the Slip N Slide mat. Annie stood up quickly.

"Hey, Father Jeff, watch this!" Annie jogged across the grass to the beginning of the mat and threw herself down again, mouth agape as she pistoled across the grass on her belly.

"Ann, Father Jeff, is trying to enjoy Christmas lunch," Ally called out as she shelled a prawn. "How about we give him a break?"

"Okay. Hey, Tammy, watch this!"

"She's a remarkable child," Father Jeff said. "You should all be very proud."

Ally smiled. "We are."

Bron liked Father Jeff. He'd been good to their family—from Libby's beautiful funeral service, to comforting a grieving Jackie. When Jackie had suggested the week before that they invite him over for Christmas lunch, Bron relished the idea. With Daniel at Carly's for Christmas lunch, it was nice to have an extra adult around.

"It's been mighty hot, hasn't it?" Jackie asked.

"Yes, yes, very hot," Father Jeff agreed. Bron watched him look across the table at Ally who sat next to her, deeply focused on shelling a prawn. His gaze raked over Ally's tattooed sleeve. "And how has life outside been to you, Ally?" he ventured.

Ally reached across the table for the Thousand Island dressing. "Pretty hot, Father, especially when we've got an outside paint job. I forgot how much that sun burns."

Father Jeff chuckled. "I actually mean out of prison."

"Oh," Ally said. "I thought you meant outside as in outdoors." She dipped a prawn into the pink sauce and bit into it. "Yeah, it's been good," she said. She playfully squeezed Bron's thigh beneath the table, and Bron instructed her body not to seize in front of company. "Bron's been helping me a lot. I'm really going to miss her when she goes back to America."

Bron didn't miss the way Jackie's features fell in distress at the mere mention of her return to the States. Jackie was well aware Bron would be flying back to Boston sometime in the near future but she was still oblivious to the fact that it would be the last time. She's going to be so happy, Bron thought, deciding that she would tell her mother the good news when Daniel was back for Christmas dinner.

"Are you staying much longer after Christmas, Bron?" Father Jeff asked.

Beneath the cover of the table, Bron linked her fingers with Ally's. "I'm in no immediate hurry to get back."

At dusk, Bron stood behind the front screen door, watching silently as Ally tried to teach Annie how to brake by back-pedaling. It hadn't taken long for Annie to get the hang of riding a bike. She only needed a push off every third time, and she was getting much better at braking each time she came to a stop at the front of the driveway loop, just before the hill. Bron thought of the training wheels she'd secretly purchased, hoping she'd put the docket somewhere safe to refund them. She watched Annie pedal away, the skirt of her new pale pink dress flowing behind her as Tammy chased alongside the bike.

Ally took a swig of her alcohol-free ginger beer. When she turned, she spotted Bron in the doorway. "I was just helping Mum with the last of the washing up," she said, stepping outside. "She's gone to have a lie down before Daniel gets here with Carly for dinner and we have to start cooking all over again."

Ally nodded. "Not sure she'll be able to get any sleep with this one yahooing."

Bron sat down on the front step. "Don't worry. Mum could sleep through a stampede."

Ally sat beside her and Bron kissed her bare shoulder. "What was Christmas like in prison?"

Ally shrugged. "It wasn't much." Just when Bron thought she wasn't going to get more out of Ally on the subject, she said, "We were allowed visitors for two hours in the morning on Christmas Day. Libby came twice—two Christmases in a row—but I didn't want her to." She sighed. "There'd be a bit of a dinner thing in the dining room. It was shit. Food on an average day was a one out of ten. Christmas lunch was maybe a two and a half at best."

Bron smiled sympathetically. "You don't talk about prison very often."

"Well, it wasn't exactly a nice experience, babe. I mean, sure, it could have been a lot worse. But I just wanted to come home." She picked at the label on her glass bottle. "Lately I've been thinking that maybe life handed me a bad go for a while so I could have all of this." She inclined her head in Annie's direction before focusing her gaze on Bron. "So that I could be really happy, you know?"

Bron paused. "Do I make you happy?"

"Yeah," Ally said hoarsely. "You make me happy."

"Good."

"What about me?" Ally asked tentatively.

Bron wrapped her arms around herself, rubbing at her upper arms. It was cooling down. "What about you?"

Ally rolled her eyes. "Do I make you happy?"

Bron leaned forward and pressed a soft kiss to Ally's cheek. "You make me very happy."

Across the circular driveway, Annie was on her way back toward them. Bron reached over and took the ginger beer from Ally's hands. She grinned as she took a swig.

Ally scoffed. "Are we sharing now?" she wondered, lightly nudging Bron with her elbow.

Bron looked out across the driveway—at Annie, at Tammy, at her beat-up Toyota. She smiled. "I suppose we are."

Bella Books, Inc.

Women. Books. Even Better Together.

P.O. Box 10543
Tallahassee, FL 32302

Phone: 800-729-4992
www.bellabooks.com